Pursuing Amy

MARILYN KAYE

BANTAM BOOKS

NEW YORK • TORONTO • LONDON • SYDNEY • AUCKLAND

P9-CLB-315

RL 5.5, 008–012
PURSUING AMY
A Bantam Skylark Book/November 1998

Skylark Books is a registered trademark of Bantam Books, a division of Bantam Doubleday Dell Publishing Group, Inc. Registered in U.S. Patent and Trademark Office and elsewhere.

All rights reserved.
Text copyright © 1998 by Marilyn Kaye.
Cover art © 1998 by Craig White.

No part of this book may be reproduced or transmitted in any form or by any means, electronic or mechanical, including photocopying, recording, or by any information storage and retrieval system, without permission in writing from the publisher.

For information address: Bantam Doubleday Dell Books for Young Readers.

If you purchased this book without a cover you should be aware that this book is stolen property. It was reported as "unsold and destroyed" to the publisher, and neither the author nor the publisher has received any payment for this "stripped book."

ISBN 0-553-49239-X

Published simultaneously in the United States and Canada.

Bantam Books are published by Bantam Books, a division of Bantam Doubleday Dell Publishing Group, Inc. Its trademark, consisting of the words "Bantam Books" and the portrayal of a rooster, is Registered in U.S. Patent and Trademark Office and in other countries. Marca Registrada. Bantam Books, 1540 Broadway, New York, New York 10036.

PRINTED IN THE UNITED STATES OF AMERICA
OPM   0   9   8   7   6   5   4   3   2   1

To Dominique and François Clerc

Pursuing Amy

prologue

Members of the organization were not entirely pleased with the director's report.

"In regard to Number Seven, has there been any further attempt at verification?"

The director had anticipated this question. "She remains under constant surveillance."

"Surveillance does not represent progress in our investigation," a member noted. "We need to proceed with direct action."

"And with caution," the director replied. "There is more at stake here than was previously determined. We must ascertain the extent of her ability."

"How will this be accomplished?"

The director explained.

one

Amy Candler stood before the dressing room mirror, examining her reflection.

"What do you think?" she asked her companion.

Tasha Morgan struggled with the buttons of the skirt she was trying on but still managed to look up at Amy's outfit. "It's okay," she said. "The color's not too great on you, though. No offense."

Amy didn't take offense. She and Tasha had known each other almost all of their twelve years, and they could be brutally honest without hurting each other's feelings. Even so, Tasha softened the comment as Amy slipped out of the lime green overalls. "Actually, I don't think that color would be good on anyone. What about this skirt? Does it make me look fat?"

"No, it doesn't make you look fat," Amy responded automatically. "Because you're not fat."

"You didn't even look at me!"

Amy turned. "You don't look fat. That skirt doesn't look so great with that old sweatshirt, though."

Tasha started to take off her sweatshirt but stopped. "I've got a big secret. Promise you won't tell?"

"Of course I won't."

After pulling the sweatshirt over her head, Tasha faced Amy with her arms at her sides. Amy waited, but Tasha didn't say a word.

"So what's the big secret?"

"Can't you tell?" Tasha asked.

"Is that a new bra?" Amy ventured.

"It's not just new. It's size B! Mom took me to a lingerie store yesterday, and I was measured. I don't wear an A anymore, I wear a B!"

"Cool," Amy said, trying to sound impressed, though she had to smile at what Tasha considered a big secret. Amy had a secret too. But her secret was so big she couldn't tell anyone, not even her best friend.

Tasha tried on a red hooded sweater. "Too tight across my chest," she announced happily. She took it off and eyed Amy's less voluptuous form. "You want to try it?"

"Very funny," Amy retorted with a grin. "It's pretty cute, though. Yeah, let me have it." She unbuttoned her shirt. "I don't know why I'm bothering to try it on. *I'm* not the one who got fifty dollars from her grandmother for her birthday."

"And a gift certificate to the Gap from my other grandmother," Tasha pointed out. "Yeah, I did pretty well." She looked at Amy with sympathy. "It must be crummy not having any relatives who send you money."

"Mm-hmm." Amy pulled the sweater over her head.

"It's kind of a weird coincidence, isn't it?" Tasha went on. "Both of your parents being orphans."

"Mm-hmm," Amy murmured again. These days she didn't like discussing her family—or lack of one. It was a subject that got a little *too* close to her secret. She adjusted the sweater and looked at her reflection. "I like this. It would go great with my dark indigo jeans." She looked at the tag. "It's on sale. I'm going to tell my mom about it. I know she'll give me the money."

"It'll be gone by the time you come back for it," Tasha said, "so why don't I buy it for you? You can pay me later."

"You sure?"

"Absolutely. I wasn't going to spend the whole fifty dollars today anyway."

"Thanks!"

Amy felt sorry for people who didn't have best friends—the kind who would lend you twenty dollars, knowing it would be paid back. She pulled the sweater off in front of the mirror; then she noticed Tasha staring at her. "What's wrong?"

"The birthmark on your back."

Amy stiffened. "What about it? You've seen it before."

"It looks darker. Maybe you should show your mother."

"I did," Amy said. "It's no big deal, just a birthmark."

"It really does look exactly like a crescent moon," Tasha remarked.

"So what? Lots of birthmarks look like something."

"Hey, don't get angry," Tasha protested. "I'm not saying that's something *bad*. Actually, it's kind of neat. Like a tattoo."

Amy didn't really feel like talking about her birthmark. It was another one of those subjects that danced on the edge of her secret. Quickly she put her shirt back on and buttoned it up.

"What's the matter?" Tasha asked.

"Nothing. Why?"

"You look like you have a headache."

Amy shrugged. "I'm just tired."

"You're always saying that lately," Tasha said. "Aren't you getting any sleep?"

"Of course I'm sleeping."

"Well, then, have you been having that dream again?"

Amy stalled for time. "What dream?"

"That nightmare you used to have all the time. The one where you're in a glass cage and there's a fire all around you. Maybe we could find out what it means on the dream interpretation Web site I told you about."

Amy didn't need any Web site to explain the dream to her. "Let's go," she said.

"Don't you want to know what your subconscious is trying to tell you?"

"Tasha, for crying out loud, stop asking me so many questions!"

"Well, *excuse* me," Tasha said.

Amy sighed. "Sorry. I don't mean to snap at you."

"You've been doing that a lot," Tasha pointed out. "You're so jumpy! I wish you'd just tell me what's bugging you."

"Nothing's bugging me," Amy said, but she knew her tone didn't sound very convincing. "Come on, let's pay and get out of here."

Amy hated keeping secrets to herself. Especially *this* secret. It had become a lump in her throat, and it was getting bigger and bigger. Sometimes she felt as if she couldn't breathe. She wanted desperately to share it with someone—someone other than her mother.

Tasha was her best friend. Amy trusted her. Still, she had promised her mother the secret would remain between them alone. So Amy's bad moods would have to go unexplained.

The friends were leaving the store with their purchases when Tasha's eyes fell on a shoe display way over on the other side. "Ooh, look at those red suede boots; they're awesome," she moaned. "I'll bet they cost a fortune."

Amy looked in the direction of the shoes. "Eighty-nine ninety-five," she reported.

"How do you know?"

"There's a price tag hanging off them."

Tasha stared at her. "You can see a little tiny price tag from so far away?"

Amy bit her lip. "Maybe I'm wrong."

"No, I believe you," Tasha said. "I know about your perfect vision. But this is incredible."

Amy shrugged.

"Really," Tasha persisted. "I've never heard of anyone being able to see like you do. Does this run in your family? Can your mother see for miles?"

"No."

"How about your father? Did he have amazing vision?"

"How should I know?" Amy responded irritably. "He

died before I was born, you know that." She hated lying to Tasha. But if she told Tasha that she had recently learned she'd never had a father, that the woman she called Mom wasn't even her mother, she might as well tell her the whole story.

Now Tasha was looking at her with a hurt expression again. Amy couldn't bear it any longer. She took a deep breath. "Tasha . . ." But something behind Amy made Tasha gasp.

"Ohmigosh, look at that. Quadruplets."

Amy turned. A woman was walking in their direction, and she was pushing a long stroller containing four identical toddlers. Everyone they passed beamed or crooned something at them.

"They're cute," Amy commented as the baby train went by.

"They're cute *now*," Tasha said. "But I feel sorry for them. They're going to have major problems later."

"What kind of problems?"

"Oh, identity problems, that sort of thing. Of course, it could be worse. I saw a documentary about these quintuplets, five girls, in Canada. They had a miserable life. They were treated like freaks." She shuddered. "Can you imagine what it would be like having four sisters who looked exactly like you? Pretty creepy, huh?"

"Yeah," Amy said. "Creepy."

"Say, I'm sorry. Were you about to tell me something before?"

If Tasha was grossed out by the thought of quintuplets, Amy knew there was no way she could reveal her secret. How could she possibly tell Tasha that somewhere in the world there were eleven other Amys?

"No, nothing," Amy replied. "Nothing at all."

two 2

After returning home from the mall, Amy ran upstairs to her room to begin the routine she'd been following religiously for a month. She started up her personal computer and logged on to the Internet. There was no e-mail waiting for her, so she went directly to her newsgroups.

She belonged to a lot of newsgroups. Among them were Advanced Teen Chess Players, Future Nuclear Physicists of America, and Going for the Gold, whose subscribers were Olympic hopefuls. She also checked the messages for newsgroups devoted to young pianists, junior violinists, wanna-be opera singers. The newsgroups had one thing in common—they were all sites where bright, exceptional, talented young people congregated.

Amy wasn't particularly interested in the violin, and she'd never had piano lessons. She didn't know how to play chess, she had no intention of trying out for an Olympic team, and she wasn't even sure what a nuclear physicist did. She was just trying to make contact with kids who had superior skills, extraordinary talents. But not just any smart kids—she was looking for girls, twelve-year-old girls with brown eyes and brown hair; girls who were five feet tall and weighed one hundred pounds. Girls who'd been born in Washington, D.C. Girls like her. *Exactly* like her.

It would be easier if she could just post a message in all the groups. Something like "Hi! Does the name Amy mean anything to you? Are you healthier, stronger, and smarter than your friends? Can you see better, hear better, run faster, and jump higher than anyone you know?" She could get more specific: "Do you have a birthmark in the shape of a crescent moon on your back?" She could even come right out and ask the real question: "Have you ever considered the possibility that you might be a clone?"

Clone. What an ugly word. It was like something out of a comic book or a sci-fi story. What do most people think of when they hear the word? she wondered. That sheep, probably, the one that was in the news not so long ago. It had made all the papers, and it was on TV too. Scientists had created a clone, an exact duplicate of another sheep. A genetic replica.

Just like her.

Amy turned to look at herself in the mirror. *"Baaa,"* she said experimentally. She didn't feel like a sheep. She didn't feel like a clone. But she didn't feel like a regular person either. She hadn't felt like a normal kid for several months.

At first she had tried to convince herself that Tasha was right, that she was simply going through the changes all girls her age went through. She wanted to chalk all her weird feelings up to exploding hormones. But she didn't need to be a genius to realize that the dramatic improvements in her vision, hearing, strength, endurance, and concentration couldn't be blamed on puberty. Puberty couldn't account for her sudden ability to solve complicated math problems in her head, not to mention her flawless athletic performances—a back flip on the balance beam and a triple toe loop on the ice, when she'd never even had a lesson in figure skating!

At least she *looked* normal. That was a blessing, she figured. Now, if only her efforts at surfing the Web could lead to a connection with others who felt normal but knew or suspected they weren't. People who were "perfect" in every way. It was a long shot, especially since direct questions were too risky. There was no telling who else, well-meaning and not, would be trying to track down the same information. Discretion was key.

An hour of clicking on icons and reading her screen didn't lead to any major encounters or revelations. Amy was disappointed, but she was getting used to the feeling. She was glad when the sound of a bouncing ball outside her open window distracted her. She looked out. Eric, Tasha's older brother, was on the Morgans' driveway next door, tossing a basketball toward a hoop hanging over their garage door. He wore a sweatshirt with the sleeves ripped off, and Amy noticed that his arms weren't quite as skinny as they used to be.

Amy had known Eric as long as she'd known Tasha, which basically meant forever. When they were all little kids, the three of them had played together. About five years ago, when she and Tasha were seven and Eric was nine, Eric seemed to have made an unspoken pact to ignore the girls' existence, and they had reciprocated. On those rare occasions when Eric spoke to them, he was either yelling at Tasha or teasing Amy.

Lately, however, Amy had noticed a real improvement in Eric's personality. He looked better too. And it seemed to her that Eric had decided she wasn't just his annoying sister's annoying friend anymore.

She didn't really feel like hanging around her room

pondering her own weirdness, so she went downstairs, out the back door, and across the grass to the Morgans' driveway. Eric greeted her with a lopsided grin.

"Hi, what's up?"

Amy responded with her usual "Not much."

"Tasha went to the supermarket with my mom."

They had dropped Amy off on their way to the store. "Yeah, I know."

Eric bounced the ball a couple of times, then held it still. He stared at the basket over the garage door. Then he took a shot. The ball went through the basket. He quickly looked at Amy to see if she'd noticed. She nodded with approval. He went after the ball, took it to a position farther from the garage, and shot again. This time the ball teetered on the rim of the basket and fell off the side.

"My turn," Amy called out. Eric tossed the ball to her, and she stood on a spot even farther away. Taking careful aim, she released the ball. It sailed through the basket cleanly.

Now it was Eric's turn to nod with approval. He retrieved the ball and tossed it back to her. She took five steps backward, shot, and again cleared the net.

It wasn't the first time she'd demonstrated her basketball skills, but Eric never failed to be impressed. "Can you make a basket from the end of the driveway?" he asked her.

"I don't know, I've never tried." Amy took the ball and went to the street end of the driveway. The garage door seemed very far away, but she wasn't concerned. She aimed and shot. The ball swished straight through the basket, just as she'd known it would.

Eric was awed. "How do you *do* that?"

Because I'm not a normal girl, she wanted to say. Because I'm a product of genetic engineering. Because I was created in a laboratory, where scientists used cloning techniques to create perfect human lives.

What would Eric say if she told him the truth about herself? Would he be shocked? Would he be fascinated? Would he be disgusted?

She'd never know. She couldn't tell Tasha, and she certainly couldn't tell Eric.

"Hey, space cadet!"

She blinked, realizing that her thoughts had taken her far away. "What?"

"Try and take the ball from me."

Eric began bouncing the basketball. He dribbled low, close to the ground, and danced around in front of her. He moved pretty fast and kept switching hands and directions, but even so, Amy was able to snatch the ball before he realized it was gone. Then she whirled around and tossed—*Swish!*—and was again rewarded with Eric's awe and exclamations.

The honking of a car horn drew her attention. She

turned to see her mother pulling into their driveway. "Gotta go," she said to Eric. "Tell Tasha to call me when she gets home, okay?"

Nancy Candler greeted her with a smile and a hug, but there were worry lines around her eyes. "Amy, what were you doing with Eric?"

"Just hanging out."

"I hope you weren't showing off," her mother said.

Amy flushed. "No. Not really. Well, sort of. I mean, we were shooting hoops, trying to see how far we could throw and still score."

"And you scored every time," her mother said reprovingly.

Amy couldn't lie to her. "What could I do, Mom? Miss on purpose?"

Nancy reached back into the car and pulled out a grocery bag. "Whew, this is heavy."

"Give it to me," Amy said.

Nancy took a quick look around.

"Nobody's watching, Mom." Amy took the bag from her mother's arms. It wasn't heavy for her at all.

"Honey, I just don't want you to call attention to yourself," Nancy said as they went into the house. "We've talked and talked about this. It's for your own good."

"I know," Amy said. She didn't feel like talking about the fact that she was in a constant state of danger. But her mother rarely passed up a chance to remind her.

They went back to the kitchen, where Nancy took the groceries out of the bag and Amy put them away. "Amy, when you were born—"

"Made," Amy corrected her.

"You were *born*," her mother emphasized. "Remember, I was there. Your birth just didn't happen in the usual way."

"No kidding," Amy said. "What did you scientists do, anyway? Take cells from a zillion donors and pick out only the best ones to make me? I mean, us?"

"It was a little more complicated than that," her mother said dryly. "We thought we were doing something for humanity, learning ways to eliminate genetic diseases and disorders. We didn't know that the agency that funded Project Crescent wanted to create a master race of superior people."

Amy had heard the story before. "So you rescued the Amys and blew up the lab so the agency would think all the clones were dead. And you took me home. Mom, you've already told me about this."

"But you have to remember that there are people out there who don't believe the clones died," Nancy continued. "And you know as well as I do, we have reason to suspect that they've identified you as one of them. They still want to create that master race. If they could get their hands on any of you Amys—"

"They could clone us," Amy finished. "I *know*, Mom."

"Then you know you shouldn't make your skills and talents visible," Nancy said. "It's the reason you had to leave gymnastics, remember? Coach Persky wanted you to compete in national games. The last thing we need is for you to become famous."

"I'm not going to get famous shooting hoops with Eric," Amy pointed out.

Her mother sighed. "Amy, sweetie, you just have to remember that you're not like other people."

Amy grimaced. As if she needed reminding.

"And you can't tell anyone about yourself," Nancy continued. "No one, ever. Not even Tasha."

"Why can't I tell Tasha?" Amy asked. "She can keep a secret. She'd never do anything to hurt me."

"Even the most trustworthy people in the world can slip up, honey. They could say something in the wrong place, at the wrong time, in front of the wrong people. We have to take every precaution."

"Yeah, I guess," Amy conceded. "It would just be nice to have someone to talk to about it."

"I'm always here," her mother offered.

That was true. Too true. In Amy's opinion, Nancy

Candler was there just a little too much, watching Amy, telling her what to do, what not to do.

"Mom . . . you don't know where the other Amys are, do you?"

Her mother looked at her and scowled. "Amy, you've asked me that before, and I haven't lied. The other babies were sent to adoption agencies all over the world. I have no idea what happened to them." She was folding the empty grocery bags now.

Amy gazed around the kitchen restlessly. "The answering machine is blinking," she announced. She hit the Play button.

"Mrs. Candler, this is Parkside Photos. We're holding a roll of film that we developed for you three months ago. Please pick it up."

There was a beep. The next message was from their neighbor, Monica.

"Hi, Nancy, it's me. Want to go to an exhibit opening tonight?"

"That sounds like fun," Amy said.

"I have papers to grade," her mother said.

The next voice on the machine was a man's. *"Um, hello. This is a message for Nancy Candler. I hope you remember me, I'm Brad Carrington. We met at an art gallery in Santa Monica several weeks ago. I've been out of town or I would have called sooner. Anyway, I was wondering if you'd like to get together sometime. For coffee, or drinks, or dinner, or . . . or whatever."* There was a little awkward laugh. *"My phone number is 555-8263. I hope you call."*

"Mom! He's asking you for a date! Do you remember him?"

"I think so," Nancy said casually, but the faint blush that was spreading across her cheeks said otherwise. "Honey, would you rewind and play that again?"

Amy obliged. This time her mother jotted down the number; then she looked at the phone and bit her lip.

Amy knew nothing would happen while she was in the room. "I've got some homework to finish," she said, and ambled out of the kitchen and into the living room.

There were times when Amy really appreciated having exceptional senses, and this was one of those times. She knew Nancy would take the phone into her little office off the kitchen and shut the door, but it didn't matter. With a little concentration, Amy could still hear every word her mother said.

"Brad, hi, this is Nancy Candler." Pause. "Yes, I was surprised to hear from you." Pause. Laugh. "Yes, it was a pleasant surprise. How are you?"

Amy knew that if she really strained, she might be able to hear what the person on the other end of the line was saying too. But she decided her mother was entitled to a little privacy. Besides, it wasn't nice to eavesdrop on a total stranger.

She had no problem with eavesdropping on her mother, though.

"Did you decide to buy that landscape painting? Oh, I know, it was very expensive. I think his work is somewhat overrated. Definitely overpriced."

Come on, Mom, Amy thought. Don't talk about art. Flirt!

"Yes, I've heard that art investment can be risky. Of course, inflation has an impact; it's difficult to predict the economy right now."

Amy wanted to scream. Nancy was going to scare him off with all this serious talk.

Fortunately Brad Carrington seemed to be a man with a mission. A few seconds later, she heard her mother say, "Saturday night? No, I don't have any plans. No, I haven't seen that film, I've heard it's very good."

Amy sank onto the sofa and allowed herself a big smile. She didn't even have to listen anymore. Maybe, just maybe, Nancy Candler was going to get a life. Maybe she was going to have something to focus on other than her daughter.

Her mother was coming into the room now. Amy snatched a magazine off the coffee table and pretended to be engrossed in it.

"I thought you had homework to do," Nancy said.

"Yeah, I'm getting to it right now." Amy rose and went toward the stairs. "Did you call that guy back?"

she asked nonchalantly. "The one you met at the art gallery?"

"Maybe."

Clearly Nancy wasn't ready to talk about this yet. Amy started up the stairs.

"Um, Amy . . ."

"Yes?"

"Are you spending the night at Tasha's Saturday?"

"I could," Amy said, grinning and turning toward her mother. "Why? You got a hot date?"

"Don't talk nonsense," her mother replied. "I'm seeing a movie with a friend, that's all." But her cheeks were still pink. And Amy could have sworn she saw an unusual sparkle in her mother's eyes.

three

Emerging from the lunch line with her tray in her hands, Amy surveyed the Parkside Middle School cafeteria. "It's so crowded today," she commented.

"That's because of the pool men," Tasha reported, indicating groups of men in white overalls who were taking up several tables. "They're supposed to get the new swimming pool finished this week."

"Great," Amy said, "but we can't eat lunch in a swimming pool. You see any seats?"

"Over there," Tasha said, pointing.

Amy made a face. "I don't want to sit with Jeanine and Linda."

"Neither do I," Tasha said. "But I want to eat, and those are the only empty seats I see."

Amy focused on the far end of the cafeteria. "There's Eric," she said. "I think there are some seats at his table."

Tasha shrugged. "So what? We can't sit there."

Amy knew Tasha was right. There was an unwritten law at Parkside. That end of the cafeteria was officially off limits to anyone other than ninth-graders. So with more than a little reluctance, Amy walked toward the table where her archenemy, Jeanine Bryant, held court.

"Don't say anything about my new bra size," Tasha whispered as they got closer.

"Good grief, Tasha," Amy said. "Do you really think the whole world is going to be interested in your chest?"

"Well, excuse me," Tasha said. "Maybe it doesn't mean anything to you, but it's a big deal to me."

Amy eyed Tasha's chest. "Not *that* big a deal."

They both started laughing, and they were still laughing when they reached the table. Jeanine and her friend Linda Riviera looked at them suspiciously.

"Mind if we sit here?" Amy asked. That was the polite thing to say, but to make sure Jeanine didn't think she was asking permission, Amy proceeded to pull out a chair without waiting for a response.

"It's a free country," Jeanine said airily. She turned to Linda. "Did I tell you what happened at gymnastics yesterday?"

Surely she would have told her friend any big news earlier, but Linda picked up on the obvious hint. Clearly Jeanine wanted to brag in front of the newcomers.

"No," Linda said loudly. "What happened?"

"I did a perfect double back flip on the balance beam. Tasha, you were there, did you see me?"

Tasha nodded. "Yeah. It was almost as good as the *triple* back flip Amy did on the beam last month."

Amy smiled. Best friends always knew the right thing to say.

Jeanine turned her attention to Amy. She gave her a sugary smile, but her eyes flashed dangerously. "It was too bad you had to drop out of gymnastics, Amy. Was it getting to be too much pressure for you?"

"No," Amy said carelessly. "It was too easy. I was getting bored."

"And your mom didn't want you to develop an eating disorder," Tasha reminded her.

"Oh, yeah. Right." That was the excuse she'd given Tasha when she dropped out. She couldn't very well have told her that she had to conceal her identity, that she couldn't become a world-class gymnast and have her face plastered on cereal boxes. It was time to change the subject. "I wonder when the new swimming pool is going to open."

"Pretty soon, I think," Linda said.

"Can you swim, Amy?" Jeanine asked sweetly.

"Of course I can swim," Amy replied.

"I hope we form teams and have real competitions," Jeanine went on. "What's your best stroke?"

"Oh, I do them all pretty well," Amy replied, but her mood was beginning to deteriorate. It depressed her to know that she could always beat Jeanine, at swimming or anything else, but that she wasn't allowed to prove it. What could she safely brag about right now?

"I got the cutest sweater yesterday at the mall," she announced. "Red, with a hood."

"It's just like the one on the cover of *Seventeen*," Tasha added in support.

"That's nice," Jeanine said, and addressed Linda. "We have to go to the mall this week. My mother says I can use her credit card and get a new winter coat."

Amy rolled her eyes. "A winter coat? This is southern California. We don't exactly have a real winter here."

"Styles change with the seasons, Amy," Jeanine shot back. "Like right now it still feels like summer, but it's late autumn. That's why I'm wearing autumn colors." Her eyes swept over Amy's pale yellow shirt. "Not summer colors."

Amy knew that no matter what she said, Jeanine would try to top her. This was pointless. She ignored Jeanine and spoke to Tasha.

"Guess what? My mother has a date this weekend!"

"You're kidding! Who's she going out with?"

"His name is Brad," Amy told her. "I haven't met him, but he's got to be pretty spectacular. You know how fussy my mother is."

"I'm surprised your mother didn't get married again," Jeanine remarked. "When my parents got divorced, my mother was married a month later."

"It's different for Amy," Tasha informed her. "Her parents didn't divorce; her father died."

"Oh . . ." Jeanine paused for a few moments.

Tasha continued. "He was killed in the army before Amy was even born. Right, Amy?"

"Yeah." That was the story Amy had been told, and the story she'd told Tasha and still believed was true.

"I have a cousin"—Jeanine had recovered her competitive spirit—"who was supposed to get married, and her fiancé was killed on their wedding day in a car accident on the way to the church." Satisfied that she had equaled, if not topped, Amy's tragedy, she changed the subject. "Speaking of dates . . . I went to the movies with Corey Schneider last Saturday."

Amy couldn't help being a little impressed. Corey

was the seventh-grade class president. "You're allowed to date already?"

"Sure," Jeanine said casually. "Of course, I'm not in love with Corey or anything like that. It was just a date."

"Corey's cute," Linda said.

Jeanine dismissed him with a wave of her manicured hand. "He's too young."

"He's the same age we are," Tasha pointed out.

"Yeah, but everyone knows girls mature much faster than boys," Jeanine said. "That's why girls like to go out with older boys." She gazed around the cafeteria and her eyes rested on the ninth-grade section. "Tasha, isn't that your brother over there? His name's Eric, right?"

"Yeah, why?"

"Just curious."

Amy's stomach lurched. "Why are you curious about Eric?" she asked.

"He's cute."

Tasha's mouth fell open. "Cute? Eric? You think my brother's cute?" She burst out laughing.

Jeanine ignored that response. "It's funny . . . I never noticed him before."

"That's because he wasn't cute before," Linda said. "He was skinny." She twisted around in her chair to get a look at him. "He's pretty athletic, isn't he?"

"He's on the track team," Jeanine said.

Since when does Jeanine know so much about him?

Amy wondered. Quickly she tried to establish her own superior knowledge of Eric. "He's planning to go out for basketball in high school next year," she announced. "We shoot hoops a lot."

"Amy, you're such a jock," Jeanine commented. "You know, I think most boys don't like girls who are too athletic."

Amy pushed her food tray aside. She'd lost her appetite. Tasha noticed her change in mood. "What's the matter?" she asked when they left the cafeteria together.

"I think Jeanine has a crush on Eric," Amy told her.

"So what?"

Amy shrugged. "Oh, nothing." Now she had one more secret she couldn't tell Tasha.

During the last period of the day, the principal spoke over the school intercom. "I am pleased to announce that our new swimming pool will open next Monday. Swimming instruction and drown-proofing lessons will be incorporated in all physical education classes for grades seven through nine. However, before students can participate in swimming classes, they must all bring in a certificate signed by a medical doctor, stating that they are in good health."

No one else in her class was disturbed by this announcement. Amy's mood sank lower. She'd never been to a doctor in her life. She'd never been sick—but there was another reason why she had to avoid medical professionals. As her mother had explained to her, any sort of physical exam or routine medical tests could alert the doctor that she wasn't like other people. Amy wouldn't be able to get a certificate, and she wouldn't be taking swimming classes.

It wasn't as if she needed lessons. But how was she going to explain the fact that she wouldn't be taking classes like everyone else? For weeks all anyone had talked about was the new swimming pool. Up to now, physical education at Parkside had consisted mainly of volleyball and running around the gym. Swimming classes would be a lot more interesting. Amy knew that if she didn't participate, she'd be doing exactly what her mother had told her she should never do—calling attention to herself.

Her mood hadn't improved when she met Tasha after school. Tasha chattered happily as they walked home. "So, I was standing right next to Simone in phys ed when we were changing into gym clothes, and you should have seen her face when she saw my bra! She's still wearing those baby training things."

Normally Amy would have found this news interesting, but today she didn't care. Her only response was a shrug.

"Can you believe Jeanine has a thing for Eric?" Tasha continued. "I thought she had higher standards than that!"

"Mm-hmm."

Tasha frowned. "Why are you in such a crummy mood?"

Amy just shrugged again. "It's nothing."

"Amy, you're my best friend and I can tell when something's bothering you. If it's a secret, you know you can trust me not to tell anyone."

"Nothing's bothering me!" Amy instantly regretted sounding so harsh.

"Okay," Tasha murmured.

They walked the rest of the way in silence. "Your mother's home," Tasha said, noticing the car as they came around the corner into the condominium community.

"She teaches evening classes on Tuesday this term," Amy told her. Then, in an effort to make up for her earlier behavior, she said, "You want to come and get something to eat?"

"No, thanks. I told my mother I'd run errands with her."

"Listen," Amy said suddenly, "I know it seems like I'm awfully moody lately. I don't mean to take it out on you."

Tasha nodded. "I understand."

"I don't know what's wrong with me," Amy lied. "I've just got these feelings."

"I know," Tasha said. "It's puberty."

"Yeah, I guess so. See you later."

Inside the house, Amy found her mother upstairs in the master bedroom, modeling a dress in front of a mirror.

"What do you think of this dress?" Nancy asked her.

"It's cool," Amy said. "Did you just get it?"

Nancy nodded. "I decided to treat myself to something new."

"Are you wearing it Saturday night?"

"I might." Nancy spoke casually, but that didn't fool Amy. She sat down on her mother's bed and wondered what she would wear if she ever had a date with Eric. Not that there was much chance of that happening anytime soon. She didn't think he'd even started dating yet. And when he did, he'd probably prefer a flirty goody-goody like Jeanine who wouldn't outshoot him at hoops.

"What's the matter?" Nancy asked as she slipped out of the dress.

"Nothing," Amy replied automatically. Then she said, "Well, yeah, I have a problem." She told Nancy about the new swimming pool at school. "I won't be allowed to take classes if I don't bring in a medical certificate. And if I can't take swimming classes, everyone's going to think I'm weird."

"Oh, Amy, don't get carried away," Nancy said. "I'm sure there will be other students who don't take swimming lessons."

"Yeah, the ones who belong to some religion that doesn't allow them to wear bathing suits," Amy muttered. "Or kids who have a creepy skin rash."

Nancy studied her. "Amy, if you could get a medical certificate and take swimming, would you be careful?"

She knew what her mother was talking about, and it had nothing to do with drowning. Resolutely Amy pushed fantasies of exquisite swan dives out of her mind. "I won't show off," she assured her mother. "I promise I'll be the worst swimmer in the seventh grade, okay?"

Nancy laughed. "Can't you just aim for average?"

"But how can you get me a medical certificate without taking me to a doctor?" Amy wanted to know.

Her mother's face grew pensive. She went to the little table by her bed, opened a drawer, and took out a small notebook. After consulting it, she picked up the phone and dialed a number.

"David? This is Nancy, Nancy Candler. Yes, it has been a long time. I need to get in touch with Dr. J." Her eyes widened. "That's a Los Angeles area code! He's living here? I see." She jotted down some numbers. "Thank you, David." She glanced at Amy. "Yes, she's fine."

After a few more words, Nancy hung up the phone. Then she sat down next to Amy on the bed.

"Who was that?" Amy asked.

"My contact," her mother said simply.

"Contact for what?" Amy persisted.

Nancy's eyes took on that hazy look that meant she was calling up memories she didn't really want. "The scientists who worked on Project Crescent . . . After the explosion, we decided it would be safer for all of us if we didn't remain in direct touch with each other. Only one member of the team knows where everyone is."

"And Dr. J—is that Dr. Jaleski?" Amy asked. "Your boss when you were working on Project Crescent?" How strange that sounded, speaking of her own birth as a project.

Her mother nodded. "I've been able to reach Dr. Jaleski over the years through David when I needed special papers for you. Vaccination records, that sort of thing. He arranged for your birth certificate."

"I know," Amy said. "When was the last time you talked to him?"

"It's been years. I thought he was still in the Washington, D.C., area. But David tells me he's living with his daughter out here now."

"Well, if his daughter answers the phone, hang up," Amy told her.

"What are you talking about?"

Amy made a confession. "I saw my birth certificate not long ago, and Dr. Jaleski's name was on it. So I tried to find him. The woman who answered the phone wouldn't let me talk to him. And when I went to his address—"

Nancy gasped. "You went to see Dr. Jaleski?"

"I *tried* to. He was listed in the phone book," Amy said. "But the house was empty. It was like they'd suddenly vanished."

Nancy nodded. "Your call must have worried his daughter."

"But what does she have to worry about?"

"Amy, Dr. Jaleski was the director of the project. He knows more about it than anyone. Maybe his daughter was afraid someone from—from the organization wanted to talk to him. Question him."

"About me?"

"About all the Amys."

"I wish I could meet him," Amy said. She hopped off the bed and moved restlessly around the room. "This is so *creepy*. These organization people who are after me . . . maybe I should just let them do whatever it is they want to do to me."

"Don't talk like that!" Nancy said. "Those people wanted to create a master race that they could use to take over the world. They're evil."

Amy shuddered. "I feel like something in a sci-fi movie." She looked at her mother desperately. "Like a monster!"

Nancy rushed toward her and hugged her tightly. "You are *not* a monster—don't you ever think of yourself that way! You're flesh and blood; you're a human being. You're just—well, you're just sort of an advanced version of a human being."

"But I'm not normal," Amy said.

"You're better than normal," Nancy said staunchly. "That's why those people want you."

"To clone me," Amy murmured. "To make more things like me."

"Don't call yourself a thing," her mother said. "They want to replicate you so they can have more advanced human beings . . . but I don't think that's all they want."

"What do you mean?"

Nancy held her at arm's length, and there was no way Amy could miss the desperation in her mother's eyes. "You have to remember, Amy—all the research we did, the scientific notes, everything was destroyed in that fire. It was the first successful human cloning experiment, but there are no records of how we accomplished it all. They can't simply clone you, Amy. They need to know . . . more."

"Like what?"

"They'd—they'd want to examine you, like a specimen under a microscope. Your mind, your body—they'd want to know how it all works." She paused. "And I doubt it would be pleasant."

four

Rainy Saturdays were the pits. Amy was looking through her bedroom window at the nasty gray world outside. It was so unfair. After she'd been cooped up in school for five days, couldn't the weekend be filled with sunshine? And with her luck lately, tomorrow was sure to be crummy too.

Amy knew she was being negative, but she couldn't help it. She wanted to be outside doing something. If she stayed inside, she'd end up going on the Internet, surfing the Web, and getting frustrated. She and Tasha had planned to go in-line skating in the park, but that had been canceled.

The house was quiet. Nancy was at the beauty salon.

She was getting the full treatment—a haircut, manicure, pedicure, and facial. Amy hoped this guy Brad was going to be worth all the effort her mother was putting into her appearance. Amy planned to check him out very carefully when he arrived to pick Nancy up for their date tonight.

It dawned on Amy that she often thought of her mother as Nancy instead of Mom. Was this something new, something she'd started doing since she discovered that Nancy wasn't her natural mother? Did she feel different about her now?

No, that wasn't it. Amy felt different about herself, but Nancy was still her mother, and Amy still loved her. At least she thought she loved her. But could someone like Amy really love anyone? Did a clone have feelings?

Then she saw a car pull into the Morgans' driveway. Eric got out. Amy experienced a pleasant little shiver. She smiled. Yes, clones had feelings.

Checking to make sure her hair wasn't standing straight up or hanging in clumps, Amy ran downstairs, grabbed a hooded raincoat from the closet, and went out.

"Hi, Amy," Mrs. Morgan said when she opened the door. "Come on in. Tasha's on a long-distance phone call with her aunt." At that moment, Eric walked through the living room with a plate of brownies in his hand. "Eric, why don't you offer Amy a brownie?"

Eric obliged, thrusting the plate toward Amy. "I got a new computer game," he told her. "Want to see?"

"Sure." She followed him upstairs.

It was strange. For as long as she'd known Eric, she'd never been in his bedroom. It gave her a funny feeling—not bad-funny or ha-ha-funny, just sort of tickly. She glanced around curiously, trying not to look too eager. The walls were covered with posters—Michael Jordan, a Brazilian soccer team, a man in a karate pose. She was pleased to note that Spice Girls posters were nowhere in sight.

The computer was on Eric's desk, and he motioned for Amy to sit on the chair facing it. "Okay, this is the deal," he said. "It's pretty brutal. You're supposed to search for the key to this treasure chest, only it can be on any one of seven islands; and if you don't find it in time, the volcano explodes and it's all over. Then there are these creatures who come out of the water, and you have to vaporize them before they bite you. If one of them bites, you have to find a special medicine within one minute or you'll die."

Amy examined the screen. "That doesn't sound so hard."

"Are you kidding? I haven't gotten off the first island yet."

"Let me try."

He gave her the mouse and set the game in motion. Standing behind the chair, he watched over Amy's shoulder and yelled out directions. "Look under the rock, I think there's a clue. . . . No, not that rock, the big one. Watch out! Something's behind the tree, look!"

The game was harder than Amy had thought it would be. Of course, she had incredible hand-eye coordination, but she had to get used to the game plan before she could use her special talents. And some of it was pure guesswork.

"Click on the window," Eric ordered her. "The next clue's going to be there."

"No, I'll bet it's behind the door," Amy argued. She moved the mouse. Eric tried to get it away from her. Giggling, she struggled for control, knowing full well she could easily grab it away from him if she tried, but enjoying the struggle.

"Watch out!" Eric yelled. While they'd been fighting over the mouse, a massive volcano in the background had exploded. Slimy green stuff covered the image on the screen. They both started laughing.

"What are you doing in here?" Tasha was at the door.

Amy was busily setting up the program to start again. "Playing Eric's game. What's this called anyway?"

"Disaster Isle," Eric told her.

"I've got a video," Tasha announced, "starring Leonardo DiCaprio. Come on downstairs."

"Just a second," Amy said. "Eric, how do you set the levels?"

"Amy!"

Amy took her hands off the keyboard. "Okay, I'm coming." She was pleasantly surprised when Eric followed her.

"I thought you hated Leonardo DiCaprio," Tasha said to him.

He shrugged. "Depends on the movie." He looked at the videocassette Tasha was holding and made a face. But he didn't leave.

Tasha turned on the TV and inserted the tape. "Wait a minute," Amy said, watching the news program that had appeared on the TV screen. "Look, it's those babies in Iowa. The whatchamacallits. You know, more than quintuplets."

"Septuplets," Tasha said. She looked. "How old are they now?"

"I don't know," Amy said. "They're cute, aren't they?" Then she remembered Tasha's reaction to the identical quadruplets they'd seen at the mall.

"At least they don't look alike," Tasha commented.

"What if they did?" Amy mused. "Look alike, I mean. I wonder if they'd be the same inside."

"Nah," Eric said. "The bodies might be identical, but the brains would be different."

"How do you know?" Tasha challenged him.

"Because they'd be individuals, even if they look alike," Eric said. "They'd have different personalities. I know a couple of identical twins, and they don't act like each other."

Amy felt a warm feeling surging through her, from her toes to her head. She turned and smiled at Eric. If only he knew how—and why—he'd just made her feel so good.

"Mom! What did you do to your hair?"

"Don't you like it?" Nancy asked anxiously.

They were in her mother's bedroom, and Nancy was sitting on the chair in front of her vanity table. She was examining her newly highlighted hair in the mirror.

"It's fantastic!" Amy exclaimed. Her mother looked ten years younger. Just then the doorbell rang.

"That will be Monica," Nancy said.

"I'll get it." Amy ran downstairs and opened the door. Monica had moved in next door only a month before. She and Nancy had known each other slightly back in college, but now they were becoming friends.

Monica, who was an artist, had an interesting—and ever changing—appearance. Tonight she was in turquoise—turquoise dress, turquoise jewelry, and a turquoise streak in her hair. Much as Amy enjoyed Monica's eccentric look, she was glad their neighbor's influence hadn't extended to her mother.

"I'm here to give Nancy a makeover," Monica announced, indicating the big cosmetics bag she was carrying. "Don't worry, I know how to put makeup on normal people. I won't make her look like me!"

And she didn't. The look she gave Nancy was fabulous—subtle, subdued, and just a little glamorous. Amy had never seen her mother's eyes look quite so big and bright—though that might have had nothing to do with the makeup. It could have been just the way she was feeling.

"Let me see what you're wearing," Monica demanded. Nancy took out her new dark red dress; then Monica did her lips in a soft rose.

"Mom, you look great!" Amy told her.

"I'm getting out of here before Mr. Wonderful shows up," Monica announced, packing up her cosmetics.

"Oh, Monica. Stop it," Nancy chided. "He's just a nice guy, that's all. And this is just a date."

"You forget," Monica said dryly. "I've seen him. He was one of the best-looking men at the art gallery opening we went to last month."

Monica was right. He was more than just a nice guy.

Amy made that decision instantly when she opened the door to Brad Carrington.

He was tall, broad-shouldered, with lots of wavy brown hair. And he was handsome.

"You must be Amy," he said.

"I must be," she repeated, and then realized how stupid she sounded. But Brad Carrington just grinned.

Amy remembered her manners. "Please come in, Mr. Carrington."

"Thank you," he said, and followed Amy into the living room. "But you know, I'd feel a whole lot better if you called me Brad. 'Mr. Carrington' makes me feel old."

You *are* old, Amy thought. Just like my mother. But at least he had a nice boyish smile. It was the kind of smile she thought Eric would have if he picked her up for a date. As if.

"Mom will be down in a minute."

He looked at the TV set. "You're watching *The Simpsons*!"

Now Amy was embarrassed. "Not really. I was doing my homework and just put it on for the noise—"

"I love *The Simpsons*!" Brad exclaimed. "It's my favorite show!"

"Really?" Amy asked. "Me too! Did you see the one where Homer met Michael Jackson?"

"That's one of my favorites," Brad told her. "Didn't you crack up when Homer tried to do the Moonwalk?"

"My very favorite is the one where Lisa has to baby-sit for Bart," Amy confided.

They were still sharing stories of favorite *Simpsons* episodes when Amy's mother came down the stairs.

"Hello, Brad," Nancy said.

Amy watched Brad closely. He was obviously impressed with Nancy's appearance, but he stayed cool. "Hi, Nancy. It's great to see you again."

Nancy smiled. "Should I take a coat?"

"It's not raining, and it feels pretty warm," Brad said.

Nancy turned to Amy. "Are you ready to go to Tasha's?"

Amy switched off the TV and picked up her back-pack. "All set," she declared.

Brad looked troubled. "Amy, would you rather come to the movies with your mother and me?"

"Are you kidding? No way!" Amy said. Then she wanted to kick herself. What would Brad think—that she was trying to get something romantic going between him and her mother? Quickly she tried to explain herself. "I'm spending the night with my best friend, Tasha. We're going to finish watching a Leonardo DiCaprio movie."

Now she really felt stupid. Brad would think she was

one of those Leonardo DiCaprio groupies, the kind who had his pictures pasted all over their bedroom walls. But Brad just smiled.

"Hey, I won't try to compete with Leo," he said. He held the door open for Nancy and Amy and walked with them to the Morgans'.

Tasha opened the door. Her eyes expanded to the size of saucers when she saw Brad.

"Have fun tonight," Nancy said as Amy went inside.

"You guys have a nice evening," Amy called back. She thought that sounded like a fairly mature thing to say.

"He is *so* cute!" Tasha exclaimed after she closed the door.

"No kidding," Amy said happily. "And he's nice too."

"I've got the video all set up," Tasha said as they went into the living room. "I'll call and order the pizza now."

"Where's Eric?" Amy asked.

"He's over at some friend's," Tasha said. "What do you want on the pizza?"

"Everything," Amy said with a sigh. She figured she'd need that to make up for Eric's absence.

five

"Mom?"

"In here, Amy."

Amy tossed the backpack containing her overnight things on the sofa and hurried into the kitchen. Nancy was sitting at the table, drinking a cup of coffee. It was almost noon, but she was still in her robe. Amy was shocked. Her mother rarely slept late, not even on Sundays.

"Mom! How late did you stay out last night?"

Nancy smiled. Amy thought she looked exceptionally pretty. "Not all that late."

Amy sat down at the table. "Tell me everything. Did you have a nice time?"

Nancy didn't even have to nod. Her happy face said it all. "It was marvelous."

"Good movie?"

Nancy laughed. "No, actually, it was terrible. I thought Brad was enjoying it, so I tried very hard to concentrate. Turned out he was only faking an interest because he thought *I* liked it! About halfway through, we looked at each other and started laughing. People turned and stared at us. This wasn't the kind of movie that was supposed to make you laugh, and that just made us laugh even harder!"

Amy stared at her mother in disbelief. This sounded like something a couple of kids would do, not two adults.

"So we left," Nancy continued, "and we went to an Italian restaurant just next to the theater." She started laughing.

"What's so funny about that?"

"I ordered ravioli, but the waiter said they were out of it. So I ordered eggplant parmigiana, and Brad asked for lasagna. The waiter took the order but then came back to say the kitchen was out of lasagna. So Brad ordered the same thing I was having. Five minutes later, the waiter comes back to tell us they just ran out of eggplant!"

Amy didn't get it. "So you saw a bad movie and you

couldn't get anything to eat in a restaurant. That doesn't sound like such a great date to me."

"It probably would have been a disaster if I'd been with anyone other than Brad," Nancy agreed. "But he's very easygoing, and he has a great sense of humor. We ended up having a pizza, so we didn't starve. And we spent the time getting to know each other."

"What's he like?" Amy asked.

"Well, he owns a small computer company, very high-tech. He tried to explain it to me, and I didn't understand a word he was saying. Then he asked about my work, and of course he knows absolutely nothing about biology, so we agreed not to talk about work."

"So what did you talk about?"

"Oh, just about everything. He told me he'd been married once, when he was younger, but they divorced and there were no kids."

"What did you tell him about yourself?"

Nancy's smile faded slightly. "Oh, what I tell everyone. That I was married to a man who was killed in an accident just before our child was born."

"You didn't tell him about me."

"Of course not, Amy!"

"But what if you and Brad get serious? Will you tell him about me then?"

"Amy, I don't think we need to worry about that just

yet. It was only a date. All I know about him is that he has a German shepherd, he likes to ride horses, and he's into food."

"That's all you found out?"

"Well, I know that he jogs. Not because he's some kind of fitness buff, though. He jogs because he likes to eat, and the more he jogs the more he can eat!"

Amy's brow puckered. "He likes to eat. . . ."

"Why are you frowning?"

"No offense, Mom, but you're not exactly into cooking."

Nancy grinned. "I don't need to be. *He's* practically a gourmet chef!"

"Wow," Amy breathed. "How did the date end? Did you kiss him? Did he ask you out again?"

Now Nancy was laughing. "You sound like you're the mother and I'm the daughter."

Amy thought about Eric. "Maybe you'll be asking me those questions sometime soon."

"Oh, really?" Interest and concern simultaneously crossed Nancy's face. Fortunately the phone rang and Amy was spared an interrogation. Nancy picked it up.

"Hello? Hi, Brad."

Amy beamed. This was a good sign. He was calling the morning after their date. Nancy was listening and smiling, and then she said, "That sounds like fun. Let me ask her; she's right here." She put the phone down.

"Amy, would you like to go to the county museum this afternoon?"

"With you and Brad?"

Her mother nodded.

"Wouldn't you rather be alone with him?"

Nancy rolled her eyes and brought the phone back to her ear. "She'd love to, Brad. Fine, see you then." She hung up the phone. "He's picking us up in an hour."

"Are you sure he wants me along?" Amy asked her.

"Absolutely. He wants to get to know you. He told me last night that one of his biggest regrets in life was not having any children."

Amy ran upstairs to change her clothes. As she did, she thought about what her mother had just said. So Brad wished he had kids. . . . Well, it wasn't too late. She didn't think her mother was too old to have children, and Amy had always wished she had a little brother or sister and . . . She stopped and smiled at the way her thoughts were running wild. Her mother and Brad had only had their first date yesterday, and already she was planning a marriage and children for them!

Amy was coming down the stairs when the doorbell rang. She ran to the door and opened it. But it wasn't Brad who was standing there. It was a young guy in a uniform.

"I have a special delivery for"—he looked at the envelope he was carrying—"Mrs. Candler."

Amy heard her mother approaching from behind. "Brad?" When Nancy saw the young man, she stopped. "Yes?"

"Mrs. Candler? I have a special delivery for you."

Nancy took the large envelope, signed the pad the man thrust toward her, and closed the door. "Amy, you know better than to open the door before you know who's there," she murmured as she tore the envelope open.

Amy expected her mother to throw more of a fit, to make her promise a hundred times to never do it again. But something—or someone—other than her daughter was occupying her mind. Amy was feeling better and better about the prospects of this relationship.

She watched as her mother pulled a piece of paper out of the envelope and read it. A small smile crossed her face. She folded the note and put it in her jeans pocket. Then she took out a larger, more official-looking document. She studied it, then silently handed it to Amy.

It was a medical certificate declaring that Amy was physically fit and capable of taking swimming lessons. It was signed *J. R. Jaleski, M.D.*

"That was fast," Amy said.

"Dr. J is not the kind of man who puts things off," Nancy said.

Amy didn't have time to study the document. The

doorbell rang, and this time it was Brad. "Everyone ready for a little culture?" he asked.

Amy wasn't bothered by the fact that during the drive to the museum her mother and Brad spent more time talking to each other than to her. All she could think about was what a good-looking couple they made, and how nice it was to hear her mother laughing. And she liked the way Brad looked at Nancy. Amy closed her eyes and wondered if Eric would ever look at her like that.

"Uh-oh," Brad said. Amy opened her eyes. A chain blocked their car from entering the parking lot. And a big sign proclaimed that the museum was closed for renovation.

"Oh, dear," Nancy sighed.

"Let's look on the bright side," Brad said. "They say bad things come in threes. We went to a terrible movie, we had problems getting fed at a restaurant, and now the museum is closed. This means that from now on all our dates will be perfect."

Any disappointment Amy felt about missing out on a museum visit was more than made up for by one word. *Dates*—plural! Brad was clearly interested in her mother.

"Anyone have any bright ideas what we can do now?" he asked.

"I have," Nancy said. "The zoo isn't far from here."

Amy wanted to scream. Was her mother determined to blow this relationship? The zoo! Nancy Candler had to be the only adult on earth who absolutely loved the zoo.

Or maybe not. Brad's face lit up. "You like the zoo? Me too! I go all the time!"

Amy agreed to the plan, although she wasn't a huge fan of this zoo, or any zoo for that matter. Even when animals weren't cooped up in tiny cages, she couldn't imagine they were very happy being away from their natural habitats. And if they had real feelings, they couldn't love being gawked at.

But Brad turned the trip into a whole new experience. "Do you ever wonder what it would be like if animals ruled the world?" he asked Amy as the three of them wandered around the grounds. "Like, what kind of jobs they'd have?"

Amy considered this. "I've always thought penguins looked like waiters in a fancy restaurant."

"Exactly," Brad said. "And don't you think lions seem like the types who would run big multinational corporations?"

Nancy suggested owls as professors, lizards as police officers, and it was generally agreed upon that birds would be the entertainers. "Or maybe monkeys," Amy said, watching one climb a tree.

"Except that's not a monkey," Brad told her. "It's an orangutan. And you see that fellow over there? That's a white-fronted marmoset."

Amy was impressed. "You really do like the zoo."

He grinned. "Did you think I was just saying that to impress your mother?"

They had a great day, and Brad insisted on taking them out to dinner. After what her mother had said about Brad's being a gourmet chef, Amy was afraid he'd take them to some fancy place with the kind of unpronounceable food that she didn't much like. But no—Brad knew where they could get the best bacon cheeseburgers in the entire city of Los Angeles. The crispiest french fries too. By the end of the evening, Amy fervently hoped her mother was falling for Brad. Because Amy certainly had.

"He's so cool," she told Tasha on the way to school the next morning. "I know he must be older than my mom, but he still knows how to have fun."

"Great," Tasha said. "Maybe you're going to get a new father."

"Oh, come on. They haven't known each other a week yet," Amy chided, but the image wasn't at all unpleasant.

"Would that be okay with you?" Tasha asked.

"I mean, would you feel like your mother's being disloyal?"

"Disloyal to who?"

"Your real father! You must be thinking about him."

"Oh! No, not really. I mean, it's not like I ever knew him." This was the kind of thing that bothered her. How much more comfortable she'd be if she could say something like "It's not like he ever really existed."

Suddenly she stopped. "Oh, no."

"What?"

"I forgot something. I have to run home and get it. Wait for me."

"We'll be late!" Tasha wailed, but Amy took off at top speed. Less than a minute later, she burst into the house.

"I forgot my medical certificate," she announced to her mother. She snatched the paper off the kitchen table.

"Don't run so fast," Nancy called, but Amy was already out of the house and halfway down the block. Returning, she was pleased to see that Eric had joined his sister.

"Boy, you can really run," Eric said in admiration. "And you're not even out of breath."

Amy felt herself go a little pink. "Thanks," she said.

"What's that?" Tasha asked, looking at the paper in her hands.

"My medical certificate, so I can take swimming. Don't you have one?"

"Yeah, it's in my backpack." She looked at Amy's paper. Then she exclaimed, "You found him!"

"Huh?"

"Dr. Jaleski, the doctor who signed your birth certificate! Remember we went looking for him when you had to do that autobiography assignment? What did he say when you talked to him? Did he tell you anything about when you were born?"

Amy couldn't blame Tasha for these questions. Both Tasha and Eric had accompanied Amy in her search to find out more about her birth. She still couldn't answer any of Tasha's questions, though, which only frustrated her. "Well, actually, I didn't meet him."

"What do you mean? This paper says he gave you a checkup. You had to meet him!"

Amy tried to think of an excuse. "It wasn't him exactly; it was his nurse who gave me the checkup."

"Then why didn't the nurse sign the certificate?"

"For crying out loud, Tasha," Eric said, "you don't have to cross-examine her!"

"Thank you," Amy said to him.

"Excuse me," Tasha said in a huff. She barely said a word the rest of the way to school.

A few hours later, Amy was wondering if she'd done the right thing by insisting on the certificate. She sat shivering on a bench with other girls dressed in identical ugly bathing suits provided by the school, and the thick smell of chlorine tickled her nose.

The phys ed teacher blew her whistle. "Today I'll determine what level swimming class you'll be placed in. You'll be tested in groups of four, and I'll give you instructions once you're in the water. Just do what you feel comfortable doing, because you don't want to be placed in a level that's too difficult for you. No showing off!"

At least everyone was getting the same advice Amy had received that morning from her mother. The teacher called out four names, and four girls rose from the bench and went to the water. One did a sloppy dive, two jumped, and one sat down on the side of the pool and eased herself in. Once they were all in the water, they began squealing and splashing each other. The teacher blew her whistle again.

"Stop that at once! This is serious business, girls."

School always takes the fun out of everything, Amy thought. She watched the girls in the pool as the teacher began calling out instructions.

Amy had learned to swim as a child, long before she knew she had special abilities. It was hard to imagine that anyone growing up so close to the Pacific Ocean wouldn't know how to swim. So she was surprised to see how poorly a lot of the girls did as the teacher called out the directions. Most of them didn't seem to know the different strokes or how to kick their legs straight. Some of them couldn't even bear to put their heads under water, while others gasped every time they came up for a breath. Ultimately they all made it from one end of the pool to the other, but most of them looked pretty sad.

Amy knew she could swim better than that without even trying. And if she actually tried . . . She smiled at the image of her teacher watching in shock as Amy crossed the pool as if she was in an Olympic race. But she couldn't do that, of course. She needed to be just like everyone else.

So when her name was called, she slipped into the water as awkwardly as the others. The teacher asked them to use the breaststroke. Amy flapped her arms wildly. But she didn't want to look too pathetic, so she did a couple of moves properly and kept her eyes on the others in the pool, making sure she didn't outdo them.

She knew she'd behaved appropriately when she received her level assignment—level three. Since there were five levels, that meant she was right smack in the middle. Her mother would be pleased.

But Tasha was surprised. "You're in three? I can't

believe it!" The girls were standing just outside the school exit.

"Why can't you believe it?" Amy asked.

"Because *I'm* in three. And you're a much better athlete than I am."

"Not in swimming," Amy said.

"That's a lie," Tasha said. "I saw you swimming last summer when we spent that Sunday at my cousin's pool."

Amy just shrugged. She couldn't think of a way to explain the sudden disappearance of her swimming skills. It was getting very irritating the way Tasha was constantly questioning her. Secrets were hard enough to keep without people bugging you.

"Maybe you just weren't up for swimming today," Tasha said. "You could ask to take the test over."

"I don't want to take the test over!" Amy snapped. "For crying out loud, Tasha, I'm in level three. And that's it, okay?" Instantly she regretted her tone. "Sorry. I guess I'm in one of my moods."

"Surprise, surprise," Tasha muttered.

Amy tried to make up for her attitude. "You want to come over to my place and watch videos?"

"I'm waiting for my mother to pick me up," Tasha replied. "It's Monday, remember? I've got gymnastics."

"Oh, right."

Tasha looked at her curiously. "Are you ever coming back to gymnastics?"

"My mother won't let me, you know that."

"Oh, come on," Tasha said. "You know you can get anything you want if you try hard enough. If you bugged your mother about this, she'd let you come back."

"Well, maybe I just don't want to bug her," Amy said.

"Why not?"

"Because maybe I don't like bugging people the way you like bugging people!"

"I don't bug people!"

"You're bugging me right now," Amy said.

"Well, your moods are bugging me!" Tasha retorted.

"Shhh, keep your voice down," Amy whispered. "Jeanine's coming this way."

Tasha made a face. "Her mother called my mother last night to ask if we could give Jeanine a ride to gymnastics."

"Lucky you."

Tasha nodded sadly. At least they could still agree about something.

"Did you guys have your swimming test today?" Jeanine asked.

"Of course we had our swimming test," Amy said. "All the seventh-graders had their tests today."

Jeanine casually examined her fingernails. "I was placed in level five. That's the highest, you know."

"We know," Tasha said.

"What group are you in?" Jeanine asked.

Tasha looked at Amy; then Amy answered for them. "We're both in three."

Jeanine could accept that Tasha had only made it into the third level, but she looked at Amy with surprise. And pleasure. "Really? I thought you knew how to swim."

"I do know how to swim."

"But not that well, I guess," Jeanine said. She smiled. "You know, Amy, living in southern California, so close to the ocean, it's important to swim well. So I hope you pay attention in these classes. And if you need any special help, just let me know."

"Here comes my mother," Tasha announced as Mrs. Morgan pulled up. This was fortunate for Jeanine, because Amy was just about to scratch her eyes out.

Amy was still seething when she arrived home. And going through her usual ritual on the Internet with no success didn't help.

"Amy, are you all right?" her mother asked when she called that afternoon. "You sound like you're in a bad mood."

"I'm fine," Amy replied, trying to sound more cheerful.

"Well, good. I just wanted to make sure you were home. I'm coming by now to pick you up."

"Where are we going?"

"It's a surprise. I'll be there in a few minutes." Nancy hung up.

A surprise. Now, that sounded interesting, but Amy couldn't imagine what it could be. Maybe Brad was with her and they were all going someplace.

But her mother showed up alone. Amy got into the car, and Nancy asked her how her day had been. Amy told her about the swimming test and how she'd managed to get placed right in the middle. Her mother nodded, but Amy didn't think she'd heard a word Amy had said. She was staring straight ahead, her hands gripping the steering wheel tightly.

"What's going on?" Amy asked her.

"Honey, don't ask questions. You'll see."

Amy thought her mother was behaving very mysteriously, but she knew there was no point in asking any more questions. Nancy had that determined look on her face. Amy glanced out the window and saw that they were heading in the direction of downtown L.A. She wondered if Brad's computer company was there.

Her mother pulled the car into an underground parking lot between two office towers and handed the keys to a valet. Amy followed her into an elevator, which brought them up from the subterranean garage to the lobby of the building. But apparently they weren't visiting any office there; her mother led her out the main doors to the street.

It was around five o'clock, so the streets were crowded with people leaving their jobs. They crossed the street and went directly to a taxi that was waiting at the corner.

"Are you here for Mrs. Jones?" Nancy asked the driver. He nodded. She opened the back door and ushered Amy in.

Who is Mrs. Jones? Amy wondered. But a look from her mother told her to keep her mouth shut. Nancy instructed the driver to take them to a particular street corner. As they rode, she turned around every now and then, as if checking to see what was behind them.

Now Amy was getting nervous. She looked at her mother, and her mother smiled slightly. That reassured her somewhat. Actually Nancy's face bore a very odd expression—a sort of tense excitement.

The taxi stopped at the designated corner. As Nancy paid the driver, Amy looked around. The area was completely unfamiliar to her. Was this where Brad's office was? And why had they taken a taxi here? Why hadn't they just driven the whole way?

But it appeared that this wasn't their final destination. They joined a small group of people at a bus stop.

When the bus came, they got on. Amy noticed that her mother was looking around again, this time at the other passengers. Did she expect to recognize somebody? Whomever she was hoping—or not hoping—to see wasn't there.

They were on the bus for fifteen minutes. When they got off, they were outside the downtown area, in a residential neighborhood made up of neat bungalows on small plots of land. Except for a couple of kids riding bicycles, there was no one around.

Nancy seemed to be breathing easier. "Now can you tell me what's going on?" Amy asked her.

Her mother pulled a map out of her bag and studied it. Then she looked at the street signs. "This way," announced Nancy. She took Amy's hand, and Amy made no effort to pull away. They walked down one street, turned to the right and walked two more blocks, then turned to the left. Now Nancy was studying the numbers on the houses they passed. She stopped in front of one.

"This is it," she said softly.

"This is what?" Amy asked.

They went to the door and Nancy rapped lightly. A younger woman answered the door. "Hello, Mary," Nancy said.

The woman nodded. "Nancy, it's nice to see you

again." Her voice was pleasant, but there were deep grooves of concern on her forehead. "Come in. He's expecting you."

Amy followed the woman and her mother into a cozy living room filled with overstuffed furniture and dark wood shelves lined with books. A white-haired man rose from a chair.

"Nancy," he said.

She went to him and they embraced. Then Nancy turned back to Amy. "Amy, this is Dr. Jaleski. Dr. J, this is Amy."

He smiled. "Number Seven."

six 6

Amy had imagined that Dr. Jaleski would be a frail old man. But though the person who stood on the other side of the living room with her mother wasn't young, he wasn't frail. He was tall, but he wasn't really thin—more like wiry. His hair was white, but it was thick and shiny. He even wore the kind of khaki pants guys at Amy's school wore, with a plaid shirt. In fact, for an elderly man, he was almost handsome. Not as handsome as Brad, of course. But okay.

Dr. Jaleski gazed at her keenly. "What color are my eyes?" he demanded.

"Uh, they're blue. Light blue."

He nodded with approval and turned to Nancy. "An ordinary person wouldn't have been able to make out the color from this distance." He turned back to Amy. "Unfortunately I'm just an ordinary person, so I can't get a good look at you from here. Come closer."

She did. He studied her face. Amy didn't feel like a specimen under a microscope, though; she felt like a painting in a museum, a work of art, something to be admired.

Nancy gestured toward the woman standing there. "Amy, this is Dr. Jaleski's daughter, Mary."

"How do you do?" Amy managed to say.

The woman smiled and nodded.

"Why don't I leave you two alone to get acquainted," Nancy said.

"Come back to the kitchen, Nancy," Mary said. "I'll make some coffee."

Normally Amy wouldn't have been too crazy about being left alone to make conversation with someone she didn't know. But even though they'd never spoken before, Dr. Jaleski wasn't exactly a stranger. On the other hand, she wasn't sure what to call him.

He motioned toward the sofa and she sat down. "Would you like something?" he asked. "A soda?"

"No, thank you, Dr. Jaleski," she said politely.

He winced. "Nobody calls me that," he said. "I don't

suppose you'd be comfortable calling me by my first name. . . . How about Dr. J?"

Amy nodded. "All right."

Dr. Jaleski cocked his head to one side as though he was trying to see her from another angle. "Tell me about yourself," he said.

Amy didn't mean to be rude, but she couldn't resist saying, "I think you know more about me than I do. You made me, didn't you?"

He smiled. "I can make some educated guesses about aspects of your mental and physical capabilities. But your personality, your feelings, your sense of humor . . . what you like, what you don't like, I can't take any responsibility for that."

Amy still didn't know what to tell him. He made it easier by asking her, "How do you feel?"

She knew he wasn't expecting an automatic "Fine, thank you, how are you?" So she answered him with the first word that came to her mind. "Confused."

"I can understand that," he said. "You must have questions."

"Lots of questions," she replied. But suddenly she couldn't remember any of them. "What am I?" she asked lamely. "I mean, I know I'm a clone, but what does that mean?"

"Well, if you want a dictionary definition, a clone

generally is an organism asexually produced from and genetically identical with one ancestor. Only, in your case—in the case of all the Amys—you had more than one ancestor. Cells were collected from several embryos; they were chemically enhanced and then fused with . . ." His voice trailed off. "But this isn't really what you want to know, is it?"

Amy shook her head. She'd looked up the word *clone* in dictionaries and encyclopedias, and once she'd tried to read an article about cloning in a medical journal she'd found at the library. But even though she had a superior intellect, she didn't have the education necessary to understand it all. "It's not the science," she said. "I want to know what it's all about. What it means. Does that make sense?"

"You're a human being, Amy, made up of the same stuff all human beings are made of. You're really just like all other people. Only better."

"That's what my mother says." Amy sighed.

"And she's right. Amy, we didn't know what the result of our project would be. We were studying chromosomes and combining cells in the hopes of discovering a means by which genetic disorders and weaknesses could be prevented from developing in a fertilized egg. We had no idea how the embryos would evolve."

"Did we look like normal babies?"

"Absolutely," he told her. "In fact, there was nothing to distinguish you girls from any other infants. That was why we had to mark you with—"

"A crescent moon," Amy finished for him.

His eyebrows shot up. "But that would only be visible under magnification!"

"I guess it grew," Amy said. She tugged on a sleeve of her T-shirt so he could see the mark on her upper back.

"Interesting," he murmured, inspecting the mark. "When did you first notice it?"

"Just a month ago," Amy said. "It might have been there before, only lighter."

The doctor nodded sagely. "Puberty. That was one of our hypotheses, you know. That the results of your enhanced cellular structure would possibly become evident at puberty. Your hearing, your vision, your memory . . . Your superior skills in this regard weren't so obvious until recently, am I right?"

She nodded. "Up till a month ago, I thought I was pretty normal. Only I sometimes have this dream. . . ."

"Tell me about it," he urged.

"I'm lying down, surrounded by glass. I feel okay. I'm not hungry and I know I'm safe. I hear a sort of pounding sound, not too loud."

"The heart monitor," he said. "You were in an incubator, connected to a variety of organ monitoring systems."

"Then there's a fire. . . ." Amy closed her eyes. She hadn't had the dream for several weeks, but it was still so vivid in her mind. "I'm scared. The glass is gone, and I feel the heat. Then someone is holding me. . . ."

"Your mother."

"I guess so. But how can I remember this? I was a tiny baby!"

"You're still just beginning to realize the extent of your abilities, Amy. Memory is one of them. This dream—it was the first indication to you of your distinctive nature."

"Except that I never got sick. And if I got a bruise or a scratch, even a real cut, it healed incredibly fast."

That didn't surprise Dr. Jaleski. "You have a highly advanced immune system. I very much doubt that you will ever be plagued by illness. What else have you noticed about yourself?"

"I'm good at most sports," she told him. "And I guess I'm pretty smart. What else can I do?"

Dr. Jaleski laughed. "Well, you're not a superhero, so you can get that out of your mind. You can't fly, you can't bend steel with your bare hands, you can't see through a brick wall. You can only do what human beings are capable of doing. Only you can do it all to the max. You can reach the highest level of achievement in any activity."

"Are all the Amys like me?"

"I don't know. I presume so. You're the only grown Amy I've met in twelve years."

It gave her the most peculiar feeling to be referred to as "the only grown Amy"—as if she was part of a species, a member of a unique race of beings.

"Where are the other Amys?" she asked wistfully.

"I don't know."

She looked at him pleadingly. "Are you sure? Because it would mean so much to find someone else like me, to talk to her, you know?"

"I'm not hiding them from you," Dr. Jaleski told her. "I honestly don't know where any of them are. When we abandoned the project, we knew that the organization might not believe that you'd all perished in the explosion. If they could find you, they would. We thought it best if none of us knew exactly where the Amys were sent."

"Except for me."

"Except for you. To be honest, I tried to talk your mother out of keeping you. I thought she'd be putting herself in unnecessary danger for the rest of her life. But when she carried you out of the burning laboratory and saved you, I guess something happened. A bond developed. She insisted on keeping you."

Amy now understood why she felt so connected to

her mother. Nancy had saved her life. "But why was it so important that you and the other scientists didn't know where we ended up?" she asked.

"So we could never reveal the locations. If we don't know, *they* will never know."

"Dr. J—who are *they*?"

He fell silent. Amy put a hand on his arm. "You won't scare me," she said softly. "I know they're looking for all the Amys, and I think they may already have found me. But I still don't understand who *they* are."

"You're so young, Amy," Dr. Jaleski said, speaking slowly. "Despite all your talents and intelligence, you're still innocent. I wish you could stay innocent and not have to know about the evil that exists in the world. The organization that established Project Crescent was an agency of our government. Still, I doubt very much that the president or any top-level governmental figures knew of its existence." He smiled. "There's a lot of bureaucracy in government. Whole agencies and individuals within those agencies can remain hidden, secret—and their real motives and agendas masked by legitimate operations and leaders."

Amy nodded. She'd heard about government conspiracies and clandestine operations. Dr. Jaleski continued.

"This agency . . . it was made up of people who were

very ambitious. People who wanted a great deal of control. They thought they could attain this control if they created a superior human race—people with extraordinary physical and mental talent who could carry out their goals."

"But what were these goals?"

"We never found out. But we knew they were evil. Amy, have you studied World War Two in school yet? Do you know about the role of the Nazis?"

"A little," Amy admitted. "I saw *Schindler's List*. The Nazis wanted to kill all the Jewish people, right?"

"And everyone else they considered inferior. They wanted to create a master race. And take over the world."

Amy sat back and tried to take it all in. Her mother had told her as much, but there was still something that didn't make sense. "A master race," she repeated. "But if they wanted to create a race"—she felt herself go a little pink—"why did they just make girls? It takes a male and a female to, you know . . ."

"Yes, I know," he said solemnly. "We wondered this too, as our studies progressed. Our superiors stressed that we should clone only females. I suspect now that somewhere in the world a similar project was going on. Only, those scientists were probably cloning male chromosomes."

So there could be boys too, Amy thought. And the organization must have planned for the Amys to get together with the boy clones. Suddenly her mouth went dry. "Do you think I could have some water?" she asked.

"Of course." Dr. Jaleski got up and went to the kitchen. When he returned, Mary and Nancy were with him.

"How are you two getting along?" Nancy asked.

"Fine," said Dr. Jaleski. He gave Amy the glass of water. "But Amy's been bombarded with a lot of information."

Mary frowned. "Is it really necessary that the poor child know all this?"

"It's for her own protection," Nancy said.

Mary wasn't satisfied. "I think it would be better for everyone to simply forget that this project ever existed. I still worry that Father will be identified." She looked at Nancy. "You were careful coming here, weren't you? In case anyone's identified you, or Amy . . . I hope you weren't followed."

"We took every precaution," Nancy assured her.

Amy was only half-listening to this conversation. She was still trying to absorb and make sense out of everything she'd learned. It was all so overwhelming. . . . And she couldn't honestly say that all the new information made her feel better.

Dr. Jaleski read her mind. "Look at this from a positive angle," he told her. "With your talents, your gifts, think of what you can offer the world. Whatever you decide to do, you'll be able to do it beautifully."

Amy nodded. And then she remembered another piece of the puzzle, something that had bothered her for a while. "Dr. J—who is Mr. Devon?"

His brow furrowed. "Mr. Devon?"

"He was the assistant principal at Amy's school," Nancy told him. "He seemed to know all about her."

"That's right. He appeared out of nowhere one day, and soon after he disappeared," Amy explained. "Nobody knows what happened to him."

"I've never heard the name before," Dr. Jaleski said.

Nancy was very surprised to hear this. "But I assumed . . . well, he knew about the project, and he knew your name, Dr. J . . ."

"This is just the kind of thing I was afraid of," Mary said, visibly alarmed.

Amy gasped. "Do you think he could have been one of *them*?"

"If he didn't try to harm you, I doubt it," said Dr. Jaleski.

"No, he didn't. In fact, he covered for me," Amy said. "I mean, it didn't seem that he meant to harm me."

"And that may well be true," Dr. Jaleski said.

"But who was he?" Nancy persisted.

Dr. Jaleski shrugged. "A project as big and expensive as ours couldn't have been conducted in total secrecy. Others had to know what was going on."

Nancy fretfully rubbed her forehead. "Let's talk about something else," she suggested. "Dr. J, what have you been up to these days?"

"I've got a new hobby," he told her. "I make jewelry!"

Nancy looked astonished, and Jaleski laughed. "I took a course in silverwork and I really got into it. Let me show you some of my pieces."

He brought out some beautiful charms, rings, and pins—all intricate and delicate. Everyone admired them. Then Mary served some refreshments, and they chatted about friends they'd all known back in Washington. Amy couldn't take part in the conversation, but she was glad they were occupied. She had so much to think about now.

Do I feel any better about myself? she wondered. She wasn't sure. But at least she now knew she had another person, someone besides her mother, a very special and good person, whom she could talk to, whom she could be herself with. More than anything, she was grateful for that.

"We are closer now," the director announced. "Everything is in place."

"What about Jaleski?"

"This remains to be seen. No decision has been made at this time."

"And Devon?"

"An unknown factor. At the moment, inconsequential. He has made no further attempt at contact. The plan can proceed according to schedule."

The director was challenged: "We have been unsuccessful in obtaining any significant biological matter to date. What is different now?"

"It has become clear that positive identification of the subject cannot be made unless the subject is in hand."

There was an objection. "But the mother will notify authorities."

The director replied, "This new plan ensures that the mother will not be a concern."

seven

A my wanted to visit Dr. Jaleski again soon. Since meeting him two days ago, she'd been replaying her questions and his explanations, thinking about the mysteries that still remained, and taking comfort in the fact that though he knew what she was, he treated her like any twelve-year-old girl. It gave her hope. Maybe other people would be able to treat her normally—if she was ever allowed to tell them the truth. . . .

Amy wanted to talk to Dr. Jaleski and find out more about herself. She also wanted to learn more about him. Already she thought of him as family. The memory of his bright, kind eyes gave her a warm feeling. Maybe he could be like a grandfather to her. Or like an uncle. It didn't matter which role he played. All Amy knew was that she could certainly use more family in her life. The only family she had was her mother. Of course, now there was the possibility of Brad. . . .

A sharp jab in Amy's side ended her musing. "She just called your name!" Tasha whispered urgently.

"Into the water, Candler!" the gym teacher yelled.

Amy left the bench and jumped into the pool, joining the other three girls in her group. She set her body on automatic and half-listened to the teacher's instructions so she could continue daydreaming.

She knew she shouldn't rush to imagine Brad as a member of her family. Even though he had been spending a lot of time with her mother, and her mother seemed very happy about this, it was way too soon to make wedding plans. But their relationship was certainly off to an excellent start, and if all continued to go well . . .

Last night had been fun. Brad had taken them to a Japanese restaurant. Amy had never eaten Japanese food before. Brad recommended that she try the chicken tempura, and it was great—like fried chicken, only lighter. Nancy had something called teriyaki, which Amy tasted and thought was pretty good too.

Brad's dinner was different—there were little mounds of rice with pieces of fish on top of them, all different colors, and they were arranged on the plate in a very pretty way.

"This is called sushi," he told Amy. "Would you like to try it?" He handed Amy his chopsticks. Amy was about to use them, but she hesitated.

"What exactly is sushi?" she asked.

"Raw fish," he told her.

Amy handed back the chopsticks. "No, thank you."

Brad laughed. "I can't blame you. When I was your age, I don't think I would have found raw fish very appealing either."

He was nice about it; he didn't go on urging her to taste the sushi, and he didn't make fun of her for being a coward. Amy remembered once going out to eat with Tasha and her family. Tasha's father kept bugging them to try some kind of weird vegetable he was having.

At one point during dinner, Brad turned to Nancy and said, "Do you realize we've been together every evening since we met?"

"Except for last night," Nancy reminded him.

"Oh, that's right," he said. "I must be blocking that."

"Amy and I went to visit an old friend. We hadn't seen him in a long time."

An expression of exaggerated dismay crossed Brad's face. "Him? A male friend?"

Nancy laughed. "A male friend who's over seventy years old. He was my boss years ago, when I was working in Washington. Before Amy was born."

"And he lives in Los Angeles now?" Brad asked. "That's a coincidence."

"Yes, he's retired and lives with his daughter here."

"He must have been more than a good boss for you to keep in touch with him," Brad commented.

Amy looked at her mother. How much was Nancy going to reveal?

Not that much, apparently. "He was a great comfort to me when Amy's father was killed," Nancy said.

Brad nodded understandingly. Then he turned to Amy. "How was school today?"

"Okay," Amy said. "We have swimming in phys ed now."

"That sounds like fun."

Amy shook her head. "It's deadly. We're learning the dog paddle! I knew how to do that when I was three."

"Then you must be the best in the class," Brad said.

"I'm not that good," Amy said hastily. "What kind of fish is that?"

"Octopus," Brad said. His eyes twinkled. "Sure you don't want to try it?"

Amy didn't think she'd eat octopus even if it was cooked, and Brad didn't push it. She appreciated that.

But she particularly appreciated the fact that Brad didn't seem to mind having her come along on his dates with her mother. He didn't treat her like a third wheel, and he actually seemed to like having her with them.

Of course her mother and Brad still had plenty of time alone. Amy usually made sure of that. And as soon as they got back to the condo that evening, Amy went up to her room so they could talk privately in the living room. She didn't even make any effort to hear what they were saying.

Brad stayed for quite a while. Later, when Amy was in bed, she felt warm and secure knowing he was downstairs. It was silly, of course—with her special abilities, Amy was strong enough to take on adult opponents. But Brad looked strong, and confident too. There was something nice about knowing that a man was in the house.

Once again her thoughts were interrupted—this time by the sound of a whistle. "Candler! Out of the pool!"

Uh-oh. Had she stopped listening to the instructions altogether? Amy climbed out of the water and approached the gym teacher, who was studying something on a clipboard.

"We made a mistake about you," she told Amy.

"Huh?"

"I think you're in the wrong class."

Amy's heart sank. Had she gone overboard in her efforts not to look too good in the water? She'd heard that level two was filled with girls who started shrieking as soon as they dipped their toes into the water. Was she going to have to fake drowning now?

"I'm going to promote you to level four," the teacher continued. "You're too good for this class."

Amy had mixed feelings about this news. On the one hand, it was a relief to know she wouldn't have to pretend she'd never done a dog paddle; on the other hand, she obviously needed to work harder at controlling her skills. But it was so hard to judge how well or how badly she was doing without going to extremes.

In the locker room after class, she told Tasha about her promotion. Tasha congratulated her, but she wasn't thrilled.

"Gee, if you move out of this class, we'll hardly ever see each other."

"We still walk to school together every day," Amy pointed out.

"Yeah, but half the time Eric tags along, so we can't really talk."

Personally, Amy didn't mind having Eric tag along, but she had to agree with Tasha that they didn't have as much private time as they'd used to.

"You want to come over after school today?" Amy asked her.

"Amy, it's Wednesday, I have gymnastics!"

"Oh, that's right, I keep forgetting," Amy said. Tasha actually looked a little hurt that Amy didn't know her schedule by heart. To make up for it, Amy walked Tasha to her class before going on to her own.

"Is your mom going out with her new boyfriend tonight?" Tasha asked her.

"Brad's coming over for dinner," Amy replied. "I'm a little nervous."

"Why?"

"My mother's not the world's greatest cook, you know. I hope she's not making macaroni and cheese."

"That's your favorite!" Tasha pointed out.

"Yeah, but I don't think macaroni and cheese would impress Brad," Amy said. "He's into exotic food."

"If he really likes her, he's not going to care what she cooks," Tasha declared.

Later, on the way home, Amy thought about what Tasha had said. She supposed it was possible that Brad would still like her mother even if they didn't have everything in common. Amy wondered if Eric would react in a similar way if her basketball skills were less remarkable than they'd been. Then she wondered how Eric would feel about her if he knew she was a clone.

When Amy returned home, she found a note on the refrigerator. *Gone to the bakery. If Brad arrives before I get back, tell him I'm on the way. Love, Mom.*

Well, that was a good sign. At least there would be a fancy dessert.

Amy grabbed an apple and went up to her room, where she turned on her computer. As usual, she started off with her newsgroups. But this time, in Advanced Junior Chess Players, something actually caught her eye. A message had been posted by a girl named Amy.

Practically choking on the apple chunk she was chewing, Amy quickly clicked on the message icon and read the posting.

> *I get picked on a lot at my junior high because I won a regional chess competition, and my picture was in the newspaper. Now my classmates think I'm a dork. Has this ever happened to anyone else? Do you have any advice for me?*

The girl was in junior high school. . . . Amy knew that lots of junior highs included the same grades as middle schools. There was no last name with the message, and no indication of where this Amy lived. She could be anywhere in the world. But her e-mail address was there.

Amy composed a note. She didn't have any advice

to offer the girl, but hopefully the message she was writing would intrigue her.

Hi, my name is Amy too. I wonder if we have anything else in common. How old are you? When is your birthday? How tall are you? Do you have any unusual birthmarks?

She didn't think she could risk asking too many questions. But this was a start. She sent off the e-mail; then, knowing it could be ages before a response came back, she turned the computer off and went out. Eric was on his driveway shooting hoops with another guy. Amy hesitated, unsure of whether or not Eric would want her around. But Eric was cool. When he saw her, he waved and beckoned her over.

"I was just telling Kyle about you," he said. "He doesn't believe you can make a basket from the end of the driveway. Show him I'm not lying!"

"No problem," Amy said, sauntering over to them. She took the ball from Kyle and went to the end of the driveway. Offering a silent prayer of gratitude that her mother wasn't there to see her show off, she aimed and tossed. Naturally the ball went right through the basket.

"Wow!" Kyle was floored, and Eric looked proud. From behind her, Amy heard the sound of clapping.

She whirled around. Brad was standing there, beaming at her. "Well, that was impressive!" he declared. "I didn't know you played basketball."

Amy flushed. Now he would probably tell her mother, and Nancy would be angry at Amy for demonstrating her talent so publicly. Amy retrieved the ball and threw it to Kyle, who took her place at the end of the driveway.

"It was just a lucky shot," she told Brad.

"Are you kidding?" Eric said. He turned to Brad. "Amy does it every time; she's incredible!"

Brad smiled. "Basketball was my sport back at school," he told them. "I was never all that good, but I still love the game. You kids ever go see the Lakers play?"

"Are you kidding?" Eric asked. "I wish. It's impossible to get tickets."

"I've got a connection over at the Forum," Brad told them. "Maybe I can get us all tickets for a game."

"Are you serious?" Eric was clearly thrilled. "That would be awesome!"

Just then Nancy pulled up. She got out of the car with a white box in her arms. "Oh, dear," she said, smiling at Brad. "I'm sorry you're seeing this. I was hoping to convince you that I made these chocolate éclairs from scratch."

"Well, they just happen to be from my favorite

bakery," Brad said, looking at the box. They started toward the house together.

"Dinner in thirty minutes, Amy," Nancy called back to her.

"Okay, Mom."

"Is that your mother's boyfriend?" Eric asked. "He's cool."

"Watch this!"

They both turned to see Kyle, who was still tossing the ball from the end of the driveway. "I think I can get it this time," he said. He threw the ball, but it was way off. "Show me how you do it," he said to Amy plaintively.

Amy went over to him, took the ball, and shot it right through the basket. Eric gave her a thumbs-up sign.

"I don't get it," Kyle said. "What's your trick?"

"There's no trick," Amy said airily. "It's just practice." Eric had retrieved the ball and sent it back to her. She bounced it twice, aimed, and threw.

"Incredible," Kyle breathed. "Do it again."

Amy took the ball. She glanced quickly back at her house to make sure her mother wasn't looking out the window.

She wasn't—but Brad was.

Other people with normal vision would only be able to make out the person. But Amy could see the expression on his face. Very clearly. He was staring at her, and his eyebrows were knitted. Amy felt an odd little shiver go through her.

"What's the matter?" Eric asked.

"Nothing," she replied. When she looked again at the window, Brad was gone.

It must have been all that talk at Dr. Jaleski's, she decided. It had left her feeling a little more paranoid than usual.

They had to clear out of the driveway then. Mrs. Morgan was driving in. Amy smiled at Tasha as she got out of the passenger side. But her smile vanished when the back door of the car opened and Jeanine stepped out.

Jeanine waved to Amy, but she had eyes only for Eric. "Hi," she said to him.

"Hi," he replied.

"Tasha invited me to join you all for dinner," she told him.

"That's nice," he said.

"You're in advanced Spanish, aren't you?"

Eric nodded.

"Great! I'm having a big problem in first-year Spanish. Could you help me with some verb conjugations?"

"Sure, I guess so." Eric said goodbye to Amy and Kyle and headed into the house with Jeanine.

Amy stared after them. What a little liar Jeanine is,

Amy thought. She knew perfectly well that Jeanine made straight A's in everything, including Spanish. Jeanine just wanted to get Eric alone.

Amy turned to Tasha. "What's she doing here?"

"Her parents had to go out of town suddenly," Tasha told her. "Some emergency about her grandmother. So she's spending the night."

"Spending the night?" Amy repeated in horror. "Tasha, you poor thing."

"I don't know," Tasha said. "I'm beginning to think maybe she's not that bad after all."

"What?"

"Well, lately she's been talking to me a lot in gymnastics," Tasha told her. "And she's been acting a lot friendlier."

Amy groaned. "Oh, Tasha, you know why she's acting friendly. Remember when she was asking about Eric? She's just kissing up to you so she can get close to him."

"Did it ever occur to you that she might like me for myself?" Tasha asked.

Amy was startled by the sudden chill in her best friend's voice. "But you don't like her!"

"Maybe I could learn to like her," Tasha said. "It would be nice to have a friend again in gymnastics."

"Amy! Come set the table!" Nancy called. "Dinner won't be long now."

"I'm coming," Amy called back. "Tasha, I . . ."

But Amy was too late. Tasha had disappeared into her own home.

As Amy walked to her front door, she thought about the gorgeous chocolate éclairs her mother had brought back. They had seemed so tempting just a short while ago, but now she didn't have much of an appetite, knowing that Jeanine was next door taking her best friend away—and flirting with Eric.

eight

Amy did manage to choke down an éclair for dessert. She even managed to share a second one with Brad. But she couldn't say she was really enjoying them. And her expression must have given it away because she could see familiar little frown lines around Nancy's eyes.

"Amy, is something bothering you?"

"I'm fine," Amy assured her. Then she noticed that Brad was looking at her with an unusually penetrating gaze. He must have been concerned about her too. It was nice that he cared so much. "May I be excused?" she asked.

As soon as she was in her room, she went directly to

the window that faced the Morgans' home. Their curtains were drawn. She couldn't see anything that was going on inside. Even with her extraordinary hearing skills, she wouldn't be able to eavesdrop from this distance with brick walls standing between them.

With a sigh she let her curtain drop and went to the computer. After she had logged on to her Internet server, her spirits lifted. She saw the little icon on the screen that indicated there was mail waiting for her. She clicked on it immediately.

It was a message from Amy the chess player! She read it quickly.

Hello, Amy. Did you know that Amy is a very popular name? I don't understand why you'd think we have anything else in common. In answer to your questions, I am thirteen years old, I have red hair and green eyes, and I am five feet six inches tall. Do you play chess? Are you interested in joining an online chess tournament?

That was it. Clearly this wasn't the kind of Amy she was seeking.

Her mood sank deeper. Maybe she should go downstairs and join her mother and Brad. It could take her mind off things.

But just as she started down the stairs, she heard her

mother and Brad talking very softly. She didn't have to listen to what they were actually saying—she could tell from the tone that it had to be personal stuff. And then she heard another sound she could identify. They were kissing!

Amy went back to her room and picked up a book. But she couldn't concentrate. She liked Brad, and she was glad her mother had a boyfriend, but it still felt strange.

And then an even stranger sensation hit her. What if Eric kissed Jeanine? No, that was ridiculous, he barely knew her. But Jeanine was awfully pretty. And Amy had no doubt that she'd be doing her best to attract Eric's interest.

Amy sank back in misery. For as long as she'd known Jeanine, they'd been in competition. Amy clearly remembered when they were both eight years old and belonged to the public library's summer reading club. It had been a real battle trying to read more books than Jeanine. She recalled their rivalry in the fourth grade, when they'd both run for class president. Jeanine had won. But Amy had beaten her out later that year by taking first prize in the spelling bee.

Looking back now, Amy wondered if her talent for spelling had been an early indication of the many talents she would have later. But all the talents and skills in the world, the extra-special vision and hearing and everything else she could do, would be no help in this particular competition. They wouldn't make Eric kiss her first.

The next day after school, Amy looked at her watch and tapped her foot impatiently. Tasha was late. The crowd in front of the school had thinned out considerably. Linda, Jeanine's best pal, was coming out of the building. Amy stopped her.

"Have you seen Tasha around?"

"She's in the media center with Jeanine," Linda told her. "They were assigned to do a project together in history." She paused and made a face as if she was thinking very hard. "Oh, I think I was supposed to tell you this last period, so you wouldn't wait for her. Sorry."

Amy knew she wasn't sorry at all. In fact, she was probably enjoying the idea that she'd made Amy wait unnecessarily. Amy couldn't really blame Tasha if Linda had decided not to pass on the message. Still, she wasn't feeling too kindly toward her friend as she walked home. Why was Tasha working on a project with Jeanine? Had she really been assigned to do this—or had she volunteered? The notion that Tasha was actually becoming friends with Jeanine was purely sickening.

When Amy got home, she went to the refrigerator

and found half of a leftover éclair to eat. It didn't make her feel any better.

She was glad when the phone rang and eagerly grabbed it, hoping it might produce something that would cheer her up. She was in luck.

Nancy was exuberant. "Brad just called me," she told Amy. "He got Lakers tickets for tonight! He told me to tell you to invite Eric if you like."

If she liked—what an understatement! Amy tore out of the house and ran across the lawn to the Morgans'. Just let Jeanine try to top this news!

Eric answered the door. Amy didn't waste time with any preliminary greetings. "Brad got tickets for the Lakers tonight. You want to go?"

It took a couple of seconds for this to sink into Erics' head. But when it did, the reaction was immediate. He let out something pretty close to a scream, and the joy on his face could have lit up the state of California. He ran out to the driveway, snatched up the basketball, and began dribbling furiously.

"I'm Shaquille O'Neal!" he shrieked. "I'm gonna secure the offensive rebound!"

Amy was happily watching him when Tasha arrived.

"What's going on?" Tasha asked as she watched Eric's exaggerated antics with puzzlement.

"We're going to see the Lakers tonight," Amy told her.

"We are?"

Amy hesitated. "Well, I mean . . . Eric and me. And my mother and Brad."

Tasha's face went stiff. "Oh. Like a double date?"

"No, don't be silly," Amy said hastily. "I wish you could come too. But Brad just has four tickets, and Eric's such a big basketball fan, so . . ."

Tasha didn't stick around to hear the rest of the explanation. She turned away and went directly into the house. Amy followed her.

"Tasha! You're not mad, are you?"

"Why should I be mad?" Tasha said coolly. "Just because you picked Eric over me."

"I did not pick Eric over you!" She followed Tasha up the stairs.

"I know why you're acting like this," Tasha said. "Just because your mother has a boyfriend, now you want to have a boyfriend too. You make fun of Jeanine, but you're just as bad."

"That's not true," Amy declared hotly.

"You're probably jealous too," Tasha continued. "You've had your mother to yourself all these years, and now you think you're losing her. You don't want to share her with Brad. You invited Eric tonight so you could upset your mother."

Amy was bewildered. "What are you talking about?"

"It's a very common problem among children of

single parents," Tasha said. "You're looking for other ways to get your mother's attention."

Amy groaned. She hated it when Tasha started playing amateur psychologist. "You've been reading too many articles in *Seventeen*."

Tasha shrugged. "I'm just trying to help out a former best friend."

"Excuse me?"

Tasha dropped the I-don't-care tone. "You've got a crush on Eric, and you're dumping me for him."

"You're nuts!" Amy exclaimed. "I mean, I like Eric, sure, but—"

"I knew it!" Tasha declared triumphantly. "You said Jeanine was using me, but you're the user."

"I can't believe you're listening to Jeanine!" Amy shrieked. "You know what she's like!"

"Yeah, well, I thought I knew what *you* were like too," Tasha shot back. "But you've changed, Amy. For the past month, you haven't been the same person."

"Oh, really? Who am I?"

"I don't know! But you've been acting mysterious and you've got secrets, and that's not the way best friends act!"

"So what are you saying?" Amy demanded. "We're not best friends anymore?"

"Maybe not," Tasha declared. "Maybe we're not even friends."

"Well, that's fine with me!" Amy snapped. She stomped out of the room, down the stairs, and out the front door.

Outside, Eric was still caught up in his fantasy NBA game. Amy went home so she could fume privately.

It wasn't like she and Tasha hadn't had fights before. You didn't have a best friend for nearly twelve years without having some major disagreements. But this one was different. She wasn't even sure what they were fighting about.

Tasha had said Amy was jealous because her mother had a boyfriend. That was ridiculous. Amy was glad her mother was happy and not nagging her so much. And Amy thought Brad was great.

Tasha had said Amy had secrets. Well, that was true. But there wasn't anything she could do about that.

She sank down on her bed in despair. Just twenty minutes ago she'd been so happy. Now she was miserable. Tasha would blame that on puberty. Amy wondered if the puberty of a clone was worse than the puberty of a regular girl. Maybe she could ask Dr. Jaleski about that.

She heard the front door open and then her mother's voice. "Amy?"

The sound of footsteps told her Nancy wasn't alone. She checked the mirror and rearranged her features so no one would guess that anything was wrong. Then she went downstairs.

"Hi, Mom. Hi, Brad."

Brad grinned at her. "Looking forward to the game?"

"No kidding. And Eric's over the moon!"

"I'm going to change my clothes," Nancy said. "Oh, Amy. I finally picked up those photos from last summer; they're in my bag if you want to look at them."

"Okay."

"I'm going to see if I can find a traffic report," Brad announced. "Maybe we can avoid a freeway backup on the way to the Forum." He turned on the TV and began surfing the channels, looking for a news program.

Amy went into the kitchen and saw her mother's bag on the counter. Inside was the white envelope containing the photos.

She flipped through them, enjoying the memory of summer fun and splashing around in big Pacific Ocean waves. Her pleasure waned when she came across a shot of her and Tasha clowning around at Tasha's cousin's swimming pool; she shoved that one to the back of the pile without looking at it. The next photo was from that same day, but something she saw stopped her from turning to the next photo. It wasn't a closeup, but Amy was able to make out small details other people would miss. She saw herself in the background, a small figure with her back to the camera. And she was wearing a bathing suit.

She focused on her upper back. And yes, there it was—very faint, but definitely there. Her crescent moon. It was weeks after that day last summer when she'd noticed it herself, and it had already started getting darker by that time. It was definitely there, even back then.

Brad came into the kitchen. "It looks like there's going to be some traffic delays," he announced. "We'd better start moving."

"Okay," Amy said. "I'll go get Eric."

Tasha opened the Morgans' door. She stared at Amy coldly. Without saying a word, Tasha went to the bottom of the stairs. "Eric," she yelled. "Your friend is here." Then she disappeared.

Eric shot down the stairs. Amy concentrated on his excited face, hoping it would help erase the image of Tasha's stone-cold expression. They went back across the lawn to Amy's.

Inside the house, the TV was still on, but no one was in the living room. "Where is everyone?" Eric asked.

"Mom's getting dressed," Amy told him. "I guess Brad is in the kitchen."

Her guess was right. Brad was glancing over the

photos she'd left on the kitchen counter. He looked up and smiled. "Hi, Eric. Ready for the game?"

"Yeah. Hey, thanks a lot for inviting me."

"You're welcome." He returned his gaze to a photo. Amy went over to see which one he found so interesting.

She wasn't surprised to see that it was a photo of her mother in a bathing suit. Amy was in the picture too, but her back was to the camera. "Mom looks pretty good there, huh?" she asked mischievously.

"Your mother looks good all the time," Brad declared. He looked at the photo again. "What's that on your shoulder, Amy, a bug? Oh, it's a birthmark."

"You can see it?" Amy asked in surprise. He had to have excellent vision to be able to pick out the faint spot.

Nancy appeared then, and the four of them took off in Brad's car. The Great Western Forum, the home court of the Lakers, was in Inglewood, near the airport, and it took a while to get there. But the traffic was lighter than Brad had expected so they made it in plenty of time.

Amy had never been in the Forum before. "This place is huge!" she exclaimed.

"It seats more than seventeen thousand people," Brad told them. "And we should have pretty good seats."

They did. They had awesome seats—fifth row, center. "Brad must have incredible connections," Eric whispered to Amy. "This is where the movie stars sit." Amy began looking around to see if she could spot any famous faces.

"Isn't that the guy who does the weather on TV?" she asked Eric.

"Where?"

"On the other side of the court."

"You can't see all the way over there!" Eric declared. "Brad, would you be able to pick out a face on the opposite side of the court?"

Brad laughed. "Not without binoculars."

Nancy glanced at Amy and gave her the look that reminded her not to call attention to her skills. Amy nodded. But she kept looking around. Only this time she kept her celebrity sightings to herself.

n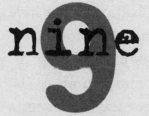ine

It started off in the usual way. She was a baby, she was lying down, she was surrounded by glass. She felt comfortable and safe, totally secure. Suddenly, outside the glass, there was fire. The blaze grew, and she could feel the heat. She knew fear. Then she felt herself being taken out from under the glass. Her mother was rescuing her . . . but no, these weren't her mother's arms. They were a man's arms, stronger and more muscular. . . . This wasn't how it was supposed to be!

Amy woke up in a cold sweat, her heart pounding wildly. She was home, in her room, in her bed, perfectly safe. She lay very still, taking deep breaths and trying to calm down.

Now, what was that all about? Why had the nightmare changed? Who was the man?

It's a dream, she reminded herself. It doesn't have to make sense. She resolved to put it out of her head, thinking the excitement of the basketball game earlier that night, or her fight with Tasha, had made her have the dream again. Whatever the reason, Amy took a few more deep breaths and forced herself back to sleep.

But the dream stayed on her mind. And as she washed and dressed for school the next morning, a sense of discomfort, of something not being quite right, wouldn't leave her. She went downstairs, greeted her mother, and gulped down two spoonfuls of cornflakes.

"I'm leaving now," she said, picking up her backpack.

"Aren't you going to wait for Tasha?" Nancy asked.

"No. We, well, we kind of had a fight yesterday."

"Oh, dear." Her mother rose and walked her to the door. "Well, try to make it up with her today."

"I don't think she wants to make up," Amy said. "I'm not sure if I want to make up either."

Nancy smiled and stroked Amy's hair. "Sometimes even the best of friends need to take a break from each other."

"I guess." Amy put her hand on the doorknob, but her mother stopped her.

"Amy, there's something I want to ask you."

"What?"

Nancy's cheeks were getting pink. "How do you feel about Brad?"

"He's great," Amy said promptly.

"He's very fond of you too," her mother told her.

"Good." Amy could tell there was more on her mother's mind. "Mom, are you guys getting really, you know, serious?"

Nancy seemed to be choosing her words carefully. "We're, well, we're talking about the future. Not in definite terms," she added hastily. "Just in general."

"Oh."

"Nothing's going to happen anytime soon," Nancy assured her. "There's nothing for you to worry about."

"I'm not worried," Amy told her. She kissed her mother and took off.

It was strange walking to school without Tasha, but in a way it was nice to be alone with her thoughts. So her mother and Brad were talking about the future. That was good, she supposed. Just days ago, she'd had fantasies about her mother and Brad getting married, about having Brad as a father. . . . Now there was a chance the fantasy could become a reality—only she wasn't sure how she felt about it.

She still liked Brad, of course. She still wanted her mother to be happy. But Brad couldn't live in their house, become a part of their family, without knowing the truth about Amy. He'd have to be told. Amy wasn't sure if she was ready for that.

All day Amy wanted to talk to someone. She felt so dreary and spaced out. She had been promoted yet again in swimming, this time to level five. She knew it wouldn't make her mom happy, but, even so, she couldn't wait to get home and talk to her mother. It wasn't meant to be. Nancy didn't come home alone. Brad was with her. For once Amy wasn't so happy to see him. She managed a reasonably friendly greeting, though.

"I really enjoyed the basketball game last night," she said.

"We'll do it again soon," he promised her. "How would you like to come over to my place for dinner tonight? I'm planning to show off my cooking skills to your mother."

Amy just didn't think she could maintain a cheerful facade for the whole evening. "Actually, I've got a lot of homework," she said.

"You have the whole weekend to do it," her mother pointed out.

"I know, but I kind of want to get it over with. The swimming pool at school is open tomorrow for free swimming, and I want to go. And then there's this movie I want to see on TV Saturday night. And on

Sunday . . ." She couldn't think of anything she needed to do on Sunday.

"Oh, come on," Brad urged. "Bring your homework with you. Maybe I can help you with it."

It was on the tip of her tongue to tell him she never needed any help with her homework, but she caught herself just in time. What was Brad going to think when he found out the truth about her? Would he treat her like a freak? Maybe he wouldn't even want to hang around Nancy anymore.

At least her mother didn't push her to join them. "You don't mind staying home alone?" Nancy asked. "I'll call Monica and see if she's going to be around. I'm sure you can go over there if you get lonely."

"I won't get lonely," Amy said.

But she *was* lonely. It turned out to be that kind of evening. Her homework didn't take long. There was nothing to watch on TV, and she didn't feel like roaming the Internet just to get disappointed. She desperately wanted to talk to someone—someone who would understand the kinds of feelings she was having. And the only person who could understand would be a person who knew what she was. She wished she had Dr. Jaleski's unlisted phone number. Well, at least she knew where he lived.

Searching in her mother's office, Amy found a map of Los Angeles. She spread it out on the kitchen table and put her excellent memory to work, tracing the route she and her mother had taken to get to Jaleski's house. She realized then that they had gone a very roundabout way. There was an easier way to get there.

Amy looked out the window. The sun had gone down. The thought of going all that way by herself in the dark gave her the creeps.

She looked at the telephone. Did she dare? Was this a really stupid idea? She decided to risk it. She picked up the telephone, dialed a familiar number, and crossed her fingers.

She was in luck. Eric answered. "Hi, it's Amy," she said in a rush. "Look, there's something I have to ask you, and it's kind of a secret. Could you come over and not tell Tasha?"

There was a moment of silence at the other end. Eric probably thought she had lost her mind. But he must have figured he owed her a favor after the game last night. "Yeah, okay," he said, and hung up. Less than a minute later she heard a knock at the door.

"What's going on?" Eric asked.

"I want to go see Dr. Jaleski," she said.

"Who?" And then he remembered. "Oh, yeah. Your old family doctor, right?"

"I know where he lives," Amy told him. "I know this sounds crazy, but would you go with me? I don't want to go by myself."

"Now?"

"Yeah."

"What's the matter? Are you sick or something?"

"No. Not exactly." She couldn't blame him for looking at her like she was crazy. "See, I need to talk to him about . . . about my mother. And Brad."

"What's the matter with them?"

"Well, I think my mother wants to marry him."

"Oh, well, he's a good guy, isn't he?"

"Oh, absolutely," Amy said. "But I just need to talk to a family friend. You know?"

She doubted that Eric understood. But he was probably relieved that she wasn't planning to talk to *him* about this personal stuff.

"Where does this Jaleski guy live?" he asked.

Amy showed him on the map. He frowned. "That's pretty far," he said. "How are we going to get there?"

"We could take a taxi," Amy told him. "I've got some money." She showed him what she had. "Do you think that's enough to get us there and back?"

"I don't know," Eric said. "I've never taken a taxi before." He fumbled in his pocket. "I've got about five dollars we could add to it."

"I'm sure that's enough. Will you come with me?"

He shrugged. "Yeah, okay. I don't have anything to do. My parents are out, and Tasha's sleeping at a girlfriend's."

Probably Jeanine, Amy thought, but she couldn't waste time brooding about that now. She looked in the yellow pages and called a taxi service. The cab arrived less than five minutes later. Amy gave the driver the address, and they settled into the backseat.

She remembered how worried Dr. Jaleski's daughter was that someone might have followed them, so every now and then Amy looked through the back window. She never saw the same car twice.

"Why do you keep looking behind us like that?" Eric asked her.

"Oh, no reason," she said. She didn't want to scare him.

When the car arrived at Dr. Jaleski's cottage, she was relieved to see a light behind the closed curtains. "Oh, good. He's home," she said.

"He doesn't know we're coming?" Eric asked.

"It's a surprise," she said lamely.

The taxi was expensive—very expensive, more than they'd thought it would be. In fact, it took almost all their money.

Dr. Jaleski was definitely surprised to see them. "Amy! What are you doing here?"

She tried to sound nonchalant. "Oh, I just thought I'd drop by and say hello. This is my friend Eric Morgan."

They shook hands and Dr. Jaleski ushered them in. His daughter, Mary, came into the room. She too was surprised to see them.

Amy introduced Eric. "I need to talk to Dr. J about something," Amy told her. "I didn't want to come by myself, so Eric came with me."

"I see," Mary said. Her eyes darted back and forth between Amy and Eric, assessing the situation. "Would you two like a snack?" She didn't wait for an answer. "Eric, would you mind giving me a hand in the kitchen?"

Once alone with Dr. Jaleski, Amy knew she had to talk rapidly before Eric returned.

"It's about my mom," she told him. "She has a boyfriend."

"Ah," he said. "And you don't like him."

"Oh, no, that's not it. I like him fine," she said. "He's nice."

He looked confused, then nodded slowly. "I see. You're afraid he's going to take your mother away from you."

Did Dr. Jaleski read the same magazines as Tasha? "No, it's not that. It's just that, well, I think they're getting kind of serious. And I think she's getting ready to tell him about me."

His expression changed. "She must know this man very well."

"Not really," Amy said. "They've only been going out for a week. But they're pretty crazy about each other. And like I said, he's a really nice person and I'm happy she's found someone to be with. It's just that . . ."

"It's just that what?" he prompted her.

"Well, she's always made such a big deal about how *I* can't tell anyone, not even my best friend. And now she's getting ready to tell this man she barely knows! I mean, I'm sure it's okay, and we can trust him not to tell anyone and all that, but it feels weird. Am I making any sense?"

Dr. Jaleski seemed deep in thought. "Your mother would never do anything to put you in jeopardy, Amy. Not intentionally. But love can make people do crazy things."

Like dragging a neighbor out to visit a family doctor and not even telling him why, Amy thought.

"Tell your mother to call me," Dr. Jaleski said.

"I don't want her to know I came to see you," she said quickly.

"I won't tell her," he promised. "I'll just ask her how she's doing and get her to talk about herself. She's bound to end up telling me about this man. I could warn her about revealing anything about you, not even to the nicest person in the world."

Amy smiled gratefully and wondered what Dr. Jaleski would think if she threw her arms around him and kissed him. But this wasn't the time. Mary and Eric returned with trays. They sat around drinking cocoa with whipped cream and nibbling on homemade oatmeal cookies. Mary told them about her job at a movie studio, where she saw lots of celebrities up close. After about an hour, Amy noticed that Dr. Jaleski was trying not to yawn. It was hard for her to remember that he wasn't a young man.

"We'd better go," Amy told Eric. "If my mom comes home and I'm not there, she'll have a fit."

Eric shook hands with Dr. Jaleski and Mary. Amy shook hands with Mary too, but she couldn't resist giving Dr. Jaleski a hug. "How are you getting home?" he asked her.

"Uh, Eric's father is picking us up," she lied. "In fact, I see his car out there now. Bye!"

Once outside, Eric looked at her. "What do we do now? We don't have enough money for another taxi."

"I know where the bus stop is," Amy told him. They had enough money left for that.

It was a nice night out. The rain had stopped, and there was a pleasant breeze. After they'd walked along for a few minutes, Amy wondered if Eric would get up the nerve to take her hand. Maybe she should take his.

"They're nice people," Eric said.

"Yeah, super," Amy replied.

"Did he help you with your problem?" Eric asked.

"Yes." She was grateful to Eric that he didn't press her to find out what the problem really was. He was a lot more mature than most boys she knew. Casually, very, very casually, she let her hand brush against his as they walked. It seemed like forever before he actually got the hint. But once he was holding her hand, it felt totally natural.

They walked in comfortable silence. Then Amy stopped.

"What?" Eric asked.

"Do you hear something?" she asked.

"No."

It was easy to forget how superior her hearing was to other people's. "I guess it's just the wind," she said. But after another few steps, she stopped again. Her pulse quickened. "No, it's not the wind. It's something else."

"Like what?"

Amy swallowed hard. "Footsteps. When we stop, the footsteps stop. But they're getting closer."

"You've been watching too many horror movies," Eric told her.

Was she letting her imagination run away with her? She concentrated on the sound.

No. They were real footsteps. Very real. And they were getting louder. Someone was following them. "Eric, we have to walk faster."

Eric still looked doubtful, but the urgency in her voice must have gotten through to him. He picked up his pace. As they walked, she listened. The footsteps behind them were quickening too.

She tightened her grip on Eric's hand. "Why would anyone follow us?" Eric asked in bewilderment. But by now he could hear the steps. His grip tightened too. "Maybe we should knock on someone's door. Or flag down a car."

But there was no time for that. The tempo of the footsteps behind them had increased.

"Eric, run!"

Amy took off, moving so fast the trees and houses went by in a blur. She had no idea how far she'd gone until she heard her name being called from way behind her. Suddenly she realized she no longer had Eric's hand and that the voice was his. She stopped and whirled around. The street was dark, and there were no street-lamps. But she could see Eric. He wasn't alone.

Without thinking twice, and with every ounce of strength she could muster, Amy tore back in his direction. As she got closer, she saw a man struggling with Eric. Eric was doing his best to defend himself, but the man was too powerful. Then, as soon as he spotted Amy sprinting back, the man let go of Eric's arm. She knew he was preparing to take her on.

Amy didn't try to sidestep the man. She lowered her

head and barreled right into him, knocking him to the ground. He appeared to be stunned but not knocked out, and Amy wasn't going to give him time to recover and get back on his feet. She reached out for Eric's hand and they took off running. This time she controlled her pace so he could keep up with her. Any minute now the man would catch up to them. She kept her eyes peeled for a hideout. When she made out the form of a playhouse behind a cottage, she tugged hard at Eric's hand so he would turn with her.

They made it off the main road just in time. She could hear the man running and panting behind them. He couldn't have seen them leave the road.

The playhouse door was open. They got down on their hands and knees and crawled inside. "Amy—"

"Shhh!" They crouched under the low roof. She could hear the footsteps drawing closer. Then she heard something else—a car. It screeched to a halt.

"She's not up this way," a voice declared.

"She must have cut through the alley."

A car door opened and shut. When the sound of the motor faded away, Amy let her breath out.

She looked at Eric. Even in the pitch-black darkness, she could see that his face was pale. "Are you okay?" she asked.

His voice was thin. "Yeah. Are you?"

"I'm okay. I think they're gone. But we'd better stay here for a few minutes."

"Amy, what's going on?"

Her mind raced as she tried to come up with an answer. What could she blame this on? Muggers? Kidnappers? Drug addicts? Generally crazy people roaming the streets of L.A.?

"That guy," Eric said. "He caught me, but he let me go. He only wanted you. Why?"

Nothing came to her, nothing that would sound even halfway believable. Except the truth.

"Eric . . . I want to tell you something."

He waited.

"It's a secret," she said. "A very big secret, bigger than anything you've ever heard of in your life. Tasha doesn't know, nobody knows, except my mother, Dr. Jaleski, and Mary too, I guess. So you can't tell anybody, ever. Promise me?"

"I promise," he said.

"You know how fast I can run, Eric? How I can always get the basketball through the hoop? You're always saying how incredible that is."

"Yeah. What about it?"

"I—I wasn't born like regular people. I'm different."

He waited again.

"You know what cloning means?" she asked.

"Sure," he said. "Like that sheep."

"That's what I am."

"You're a sheep?"

"Eric, I'm a clone."

This time *she* waited. Was he going to burst out laughing? Was he going to run from her in horror? She wasn't sure which reaction would be worse.

At first Eric didn't react. He was completely silent.

"Eric, did you hear me?"

"Yeah, I heard you."

She might as well let it all out. "I was born—I was *made* in a laboratory. Dr. Jaleski was the head of a scientific experiment called Project Crescent. My mother was one of the scientists working with him. They created a series of clones, identical girls, twelve in all. I was one of them."

She looked at him closely, trying to read what was in his eyes. Disbelief? Disgust? No, neither of those. There was some doubt, sure. But mostly there was wonderment.

ten 10

As she lay in bed Saturday morning, it all seemed to Amy like just another weird dream. The chase, the playhouse, revealing her secret to Eric—had it all really happened?

She felt perfectly fine now. It had been scary last night, but remembering how she'd saved herself made her feel brave and strong and ready to take on any bad guys she might encounter.

She looked at the clock by her bed. It was almost ten o'clock. She jumped out of bed and dressed quickly. Out in the hall, she could see her mother's door ajar. She peeked inside. Nancy was still sleeping.

If her mother found out what had happened . . . Amy

shuddered at the mere thought. She probably wouldn't be allowed out of the house again till she was old enough to vote. Fortunately her mother had still been out with Brad when Amy had arrived home. Eric had been equally lucky—there'd been no car in his driveway.

He was waiting for her outside her back door now, just as they'd planned. She motioned for him to wait as she quickly scrawled a message.

Mom—I went to the pool with Eric. She stuck the note on the refrigerator door with a magnet and ran outside.

"You know, it all makes sense now," he said as they walked to school. "Remember when we played Disaster Isle on my computer? You were incredible."

Amy grinned. She didn't think the full impact of her situation had hit him yet. "I can do lots of things," she told him. It was such a relief knowing she'd never again have to worry about showing off in front of Eric. He understood about her; he didn't think she was a freak—she felt so free!

He'd asked her a million questions during the bus ride home. He'd wanted to know more about Project Crescent and why it was canceled. He had more questions today.

"Exactly how fast can you run?"

"I'm not sure. I've never timed myself."

"Do you know how high you can jump?"

"No. Pretty high, though."

She supposed she could have done a little demonstration of her talents right then and there. But she didn't want to overwhelm him.

This was the first weekend that the school pool was open to the community. Most people didn't know about it yet, so it wasn't very crowded. Amy spotted a familiar face right away. "There's Tasha," she told Eric.

"How come you guys aren't hanging out?" he asked her.

"She has a new friend," Amy said. Sure enough, it was Jeanine who was demonstrating the butterfly kick to Tasha.

Jeanine and Tasha saw them too. Tasha turned away. But Jeanine climbed out of the pool and sauntered toward them in her bikini. "Hi, guys," she said, but of course she only had eyes for Eric. He mumbled "Hi," but he didn't make any serious eye contact with her. So she directed her attention to Amy.

"There's a lifeguard on duty, Amy," she said in that sweet, patronizing way Amy detested. "So you don't have to worry about going into the deep end."

Amy couldn't take this, especially in front of Eric. "Jeanine, want to race?"

Jeanine was surprised. "Oh, Amy, I don't think we should do that. It's not like we're on the same level."

"We will be on Monday," Amy told her. "I've been promoted to level five."

"Go ahead and race," Eric said. "I want to see this."

Jeanine looked at him uncertainly. Then she shrugged. "Okay."

She and Amy went to the deep end of the pool. "To the other end and back, okay?" Amy said.

Jeanine nodded.

"On the count of three," Eric said. "One, two, three!"

Amy dove into the water. She didn't even think about Jeanine swimming next to her. And, anyway, Jeanine wasn't next to her for long.

Amy had no idea how much time it took her to get to the opposite end of the pool, turn, and swim back. It seemed only seconds. She was kicking so fast, she felt like she had a motor driving her forward.

She won easily. Eric held out his hand and helped her out of the water. Jeanine hadn't even reached the end of the pool yet. When she got there, Tasha grabbed her arm and pointed. Jeanine stared back at Amy in utter disbelief. It was glorious.

Eric was very impressed. But later, on the way home, he had second thoughts about it. "I was just thinking," he said. "You told me last night, it's a big secret, right? And you're not supposed to draw attention to yourself because people are after you."

"Right," Amy said.

"Then maybe it's not a great idea for you to swim like a dolphin in public."

"There was hardly anyone in the pool," she pointed out.

"Yeah, but you should be careful."

"It's that Jeanine," Amy said. "She thinks she's so cool."

"Yeah, she's pretty conceited," Eric agreed. "But she's nothing special."

Amy felt all warm and shivery at the same time.

When they got home, she invited him inside to raid the refrigerator. The note she'd left for her mother was gone, and another note had taken its place. Her mother was out running errands, and she'd be back around one.

That wasn't the only information the note relayed. It appeared that Brad was taking them on a picnic to some woods tomorrow.

"Oh, I know where that is," Eric said, looking at the note. "My Boy Scout troop went on a hike there."

"You want to come with us?" Amy asked hopefully.

"I can't," he said. "I'm supposed to go bowling with my dad. He's into this father-and-son stuff lately."

Amy thought about Brad. Would he want to do father-and-daughter stuff with her?

Eric was gone by the time her mother came home that afternoon. "Hi, honey," Nancy said. "I feel like I haven't seen you in ages! What's up?"

If she only knew. Then Amy remembered why she'd

gone out last night in the first place. "Mom, have you talked to Dr. Jaleski today?"

"No. Why?"

"Um, well, he called, and . . . and I forgot to tell you."

"Oh. All right." Nancy went to her office, but this time Amy didn't try to eavesdrop. She knew what Dr. Jaleski was going to say.

Instead she headed toward the living room and MTV. They were playing the top ten videos. Amy settled back into the sofa to watch. She was so engrossed, she didn't even hear her mother when she came into the room.

"Amy . . ."

Amy looked up and saw that her mother's face was drained of color.

"Mom? What's the matter?"

"Dr. Jaleski . . ."

Amy hopped off the sofa. "What about him?"

Her mother's lips moved but nothing happened. Finally words came out.

"He's dead."

eleven

"**W**hat happened?" Amy asked.

"I don't know," Nancy replied. "I spoke to David, my contact. He didn't have any details. I suppose it was something like a heart attack."

"But he looked fine last night," Amy burst out.

"Last night?" Nancy stared at her. "Amy, what are you talking about? You saw Dr. J last night? How?"

Amy wiped her tears. "I went to see him."

"By yourself?" her mother asked, shocked. "How did you get there?"

"I went with Eric, and we took a taxi."

"But why? Don't you realize how dangerous that was?"

"Nothing happened to me," Amy lied.

"But it could have been dangerous for Dr. J! If you took a taxi from here to his place, you could easily have been followed!"

"But I wasn't," Amy said. "And at least I got to see him again before he died!"

Her mother was clearly distraught. "I can't talk about this now, Amy!" She ran upstairs to her room. Amy heard the door close—and her mother crying behind it.

It was a weird and awful day. Nancy spent most of it in her room. Amy remained huddled on the sofa in the living room with the TV on. She needed the noise to drown out her thoughts.

Could *she* have caused Dr. Jaleski's death? Had her conversation upset him in some way? Had he had a heart attack because of her? She'd never know, but she'd always feel guilty. She curled up on the sofa in utter misery and cried off and on for the entire day.

Hours later her mother came back downstairs and sat down on the sofa next to Amy. She looked exhausted.

"Honey, I didn't mean to yell at you earlier," Nancy said softly. "But you shouldn't take risks like that. At least Eric was with you." She frowned. "What did you tell Eric about Dr. J?"

"Nothing, really." Amy didn't think her mother could deal with any more unhappy news. "Just that he's a family friend."

The phone rang and Nancy got up. "Maybe that's Mary with more information."

But it was Brad calling. Amy half-listened to her mother explaining the situation. "My former boss, the man I told you about . . . yes, very suddenly . . . heart, I think . . . tomorrow? Oh, Brad, I don't think so, I'm feeling so sad." There was a long pause. "I don't know . . . I suppose you could be right. Let me think about it and talk to Amy. All right, I'll call you later."

"We're not going on the picnic tomorrow, are we?" Amy asked when her mother returned.

"Brad thinks we should. It would be quiet and peaceful, and he says it would make us feel better to be out in the fresh air. What do you think?"

Amy didn't care one way or the other. In the house or in the woods, it didn't matter. She'd still feel miserable.

Sunday was a perfect picnic day. The sun was shining, and the temperature was warm but not hot. Brad picked them up at noon. He was very gentle and sweet with Nancy, not prying or trying to make her talk about her loss. He asked Amy how she was feeling, but he didn't bombard her with questions. The radio was turned to a classical station, and the soft music was comforting.

It took almost an hour to reach their destination. "We can't drive into the wooded area," Brad told them. "So I'll leave the car in a lot and we'll hike. Is that okay with you two?"

"Absolutely," Nancy said. "I could use some exercise." With a picnic basket on a strap dangling from his shoulder, Brad led the way into the woods. "This is one of my favorite places in the world," he told them. "I don't think too many people know about it. Even on a beautiful Sunday like this, you can wander through these woods for hours and never run into another person."

"It's beautiful," Nancy said, and Amy agreed. Huge trees surrounded them, and the sunlight sparkled through the leaves. Birds sang, and every now and then a squirrel crossed their path. Wildflowers appeared in clusters, and Amy even spotted what looked like a tiny strawberry patch.

Eventually they reached a small grassy clearing. Brad set down the picnic basket. "How's this?" he asked them.

"Perfect," Amy and her mother said in unison.

Brad pulled out a blanket and spread it on the ground. Then they all pitched in to lay out the picnic.

"I hope everyone's hungry," Brad said.

Just yesterday Amy had thought she'd never want to eat again. But Brad's feast was impossible to resist. He'd made fried chicken, potato salad, another kind of exotic salad with beans and onions, and fabulous flaky cheese straws. Dessert was a platter of homemade brownies.

"Yikes!" Amy exclaimed. "This is a banquet!"

"Brad, you've really gone too far," Nancy said. "There's enough food here for an army." From her bag, she pulled out a bottle of fancy wine. "A colleague of mine at the university went to France and brought me this. I'd like it to be my contribution to this great meal."

Brad examined the label. "Wow. This is special."

"I've been saving it for a special occasion," Nancy told him.

"I'm honored that you want to share it with me," Brad said. "But it's a shame to drink it with fried chicken. With this kind of wine, we should be eating pheasant under glass."

"Well, did you bring any pheasant under glass?" Nancy asked with a smile. "No? So it will have to go with fried chicken."

Brad wasn't convinced. "Seriously, Nancy, a burgundy like this just wouldn't be right. I've brought a nice Chablis, and it will go perfectly with the chicken." He rummaged in the basket and pulled out a bottle.

"But I want to try this burgundy," Nancy protested.

Amy could have sworn she saw a flash of annoyance cross Brad's face. "Another time," he said. "Believe me, Nancy, the white wine will be better with the chicken."

"I didn't know you knew so much about wines," Nancy remarked.

Brad's good humor returned. "Oh, I'm just showing off to impress you. And check out the liquid refreshment I brought for Amy." It was a bottle of some fancy brand of lemonade.

They all settled into an orgy of eating. In Amy's opinion, everything was absolutely delicious. The chicken was better than any of that fast-food stuff she usually ate, and the strange bean and onion salad was nice and spicy. She stuffed herself.

When she'd finished, Brad and her mother were talking softly. Amy figured it was time to make herself scarce. "I'm going to pick some wildflowers," she announced.

"Don't go far, honey," Nancy said. Her words were slurred.

"Mom, how much wine did you drink?" Amy glanced at the wine bottle. It was almost full. Her mother was still on her first glass, and Brad hadn't even touched his.

Nancy made an odd sort of giggling sound.

"Mom? Are you okay?"

Nancy smiled. Amy thought her eyes looked funny.

"She's fine," Brad said.

But Nancy's smile suddenly faded and her eyes focused on Brad, widening with horror. "You . . . you . . ." Then she fell back on the blanket.

"Mom!" Amy screamed. "Brad! Do something!"

"I'm going to," Brad said. He stood up. "Come on."

"What?"

Brad grabbed her arm. "We're getting out of here." His grip was tight, almost painful.

"What are you talking about?" Amy cried. "What's going on?"

Brad didn't answer. He just dragged her away from the blanket. "Let me go!" Amy shrieked.

"Be quiet," Brad said coldly. "Just do as you're told and you won't be hurt." He rapidly moved her along.

"What did you do to my mother?" Amy wailed. "Where are you taking me?"

He said nothing. Fear practically closed off her throat as the horrifying realization hit her. "You're one of *them*," she whispered.

They were heading toward the lot where he'd left the car. Amy looked around wildly. She didn't see another soul. She tried to pull herself free, but as Dr.

Jaleski had told her, she wasn't a superhero. She might be a lot stronger than any other twelve-year-old girl, but she wasn't as strong as a muscular man like Brad.

Then, like a flash of lightning, she remembered something—a film that had been shown in her phys ed class the year before, about self-defense for girls. Frantically she tried to conjure up the techniques shown in the movie.

She didn't need to be a superhero; she didn't even have to be a superskilled clone. But she did need to be fast.

Amy let herself go limp. Then, as Brad turned to look at her, her fingers went directly to his eyes and her knee got him between his legs. He let out a yell. And for a second, his grip on her loosened. A second was all the time Amy needed.

She took off. As she ran, she recalled Eric asking her how fast she could run. She wished she had a timer right now. She was running with a speed that surprised even her. Her feet seemed to barely touch the ground.

But Brad must have been a fast runner too. She could hear his footsteps. Frantically she considered her options.

She took a running leap and managed to grab on to the dangling branch of a tree. Hoisting herself up, she clambered onto a sturdier limb and moved quickly upward. The tree was leafy; she crawled deeper into it so the leaves would hide her. She just hoped the limbs were strong enough to hold her.

Cautiously she pushed some branches aside to peek out. She saw Brad, running in her direction, but he wasn't looking up. That meant he probably hadn't seen her climb the tree. But that didn't mean she was safe. She looked off in the other direction, hoping she might see her mother. What had he done to her? Then it hit her. The white wine. Brad had insisted Nancy drink it. Had he poisoned her? Was she sleeping? Was she dead?

Amy looked back toward Brad. He was practically under her. She held her breath. Then, to her horror, he looked up. There was no way she could disappear in the leaves, but she tried to make herself as small as possible. He spotted her—and his cold eyes locked onto hers.

Amy didn't move. Neither did Brad.

And then she heard something. It was very, very faint, so it had to be far away. But it only took her a second to identify the sound. Sirens.

Brad heard them too and took off.

She waited until she couldn't see him or hear his footsteps. Then she scrambled down the tree and ran back to where her mother was lying.

Nancy was still there, but she wasn't alone. "Eric! What are you doing here?" Amy cried.

"My bowling day with Dad was canceled, so I decided to take you up on your offer. Mom dropped me off." He was holding Nancy's wrist. "I'm glad I came."

Amy knelt down beside him. "Is she alive?"

He nodded. "I just called nine-one-one. It's a good thing I know these woods and that my mom gave me her cellular phone in case of an emergency."

Amy was so worried about her mother that she didn't hear the approach of the paramedics. They immediately strapped an oxygen mask on Nancy's face and moved her onto a stretcher.

Amy and Eric followed as the paramedics wheeled the stretcher back to the parking lot, where the ambulance was waiting. Even in her distress, Amy noticed that Brad's car was gone. So he got away, she thought—which means he's still out there, somewhere. But she couldn't worry about that now.

In the back of the ambulance, she asked the paramedic how her mother was. "Her pulse is weak," the woman told her. "But she looks strong."

Stay strong, Mom, Amy prayed silently. Stay strong.

twelve

Eric called his parents from the hospital. Mrs. Morgan said she and Tasha would come right over. Amy was still waiting for news on her unconscious mother. The doctor wanted to check Amy for injuries too, but Amy had managed to convince her that she was fine. The doctor did give her a quick exam, checking her heart and blood pressure and feeling for broken bones, but luckily the doctor didn't insist on any tests. And Amy *was* fine—physically, at least.

Her mother wasn't. The doctor confirmed that Nancy had been poisoned, but she was baffled by the nature of the poison.

"Your mother doesn't appear to be in any immediate

danger," the doctor told Amy. "Her pulse is getting back to normal, and there doesn't seem to be any brain damage."

"When will she wake up?" Amy asked.

"We're not sure."

Amy wanted to stay by her mother's side in the emergency room, but Mrs. Morgan insisted she come home with them.

"What were you doing in the woods anyway?" Tasha asked as they left the hospital.

"Having a picnic."

"With Brad?"

Amy hesitated. They'd asked her at the hospital if anyone else had been with them. They wanted to know if Nancy had been intentionally poisoned, or if this was some sort of accident caused by bad food. Amy told them she and her mother had been alone in the woods. In the past Nancy had said not to get the police involved; otherwise there was no way to protect Amy. They would have to reveal their secret.

Amy answered Tasha's question. "No. Brad wasn't there."

"Are you going to call him and tell him what happened?"

"Tasha, don't bother Amy with questions now," Mrs. Morgan scolded.

"Yeah, Tasha, save it for later," Eric said. "It's been a pretty harrowing day."

Amy saw him give her a look, and she knew that he knew she had just lied about Brad. She would have to tell him the full story—and she wished Tasha could be told the truth too.

"I'm sorry," Tasha said meekly.

"That's okay," Amy replied automatically. But she did want to be left alone with her thoughts.

There was some improvement in her mother's condition on Monday, but Nancy still drifted in and out of consciousness. Doctors were busy doing blood tests to determine what kind of poison was in her system. Amy was in the way, and Mrs. Morgan convinced her that if she didn't keep to her usual schedule, her mother would be upset. Amy made only one condition—that no one at school be told what had happened. She didn't want people bugging her with questions.

Now it was Wednesday morning. Nothing had changed. Nancy was still floating in and out of consciousness, and the doctors still hadn't established the cause of her symptoms. Amy was still with the Morgans.

The alarm on Tasha's side of the room went off. Tasha struggled to sit up; then she turned it off. "How long have you been awake?" she asked Amy.

"Just a few minutes," Amy replied.

"Would you like to use the bathroom first?"

"No, you go ahead."

This was how they'd been speaking to each other for the past few days. Perfectly polite. Nothing more.

At breakfast Mrs. Morgan had an announcement. "I have a surprise for you kids. I'm taking the three of you to something wonderful." She waved the tickets she was holding in her hand.

"Basketball?" Eric asked hopefully.

"No. Ballet."

Eric groaned.

"Neat!" Tasha proclaimed, and Amy agreed.

"It's a touring company from France," Mrs. Morgan told them. "They're performing *The Nutcracker,* and they're only here for one night."

"Goody, goody," Eric muttered.

"Stop that," Mrs. Morgan said sternly. "Amy needs a nice distraction, and you're lucky I'm letting you come along."

"Thanks, Mrs. Morgan," Amy said. "I've never seen a live ballet performance before."

"This should be pretty special," Mrs. Morgan told her. "I've been reading about this company. Their prima ballerina is supposed to be remarkable, quite young and extraordinarily talented."

"Isn't it a little early for *The Nutcracker*?" Tasha asked. "This is only November."

"Los Angeles is the first stop on their North American tour," Mrs. Morgan explained. "And they're only here for one night. I was lucky to get tickets."

The thought of going to the ballet gave Amy something to look forward to all day. And her spirits were lifted higher when she visited her mother at the hospital that afternoon.

"She's staying conscious for longer periods," the doctor told her. "We haven't been able to figure out the nature of the poison, though. We're wondering now if it could be some kind of virus that was introduced into her system, but we can't determine how. But she is definitely showing improvement. It may be that she will recover on her own and we'll never know what caused this disorder."

Amy wasn't surprised that the doctors were at a loss to explain the strange illness. She was sure Brad and the people he worked for had sophisticated means at their disposal. After all, these were the same people who understood the secrets of cloning.

Nancy didn't look all that sick today. She was pale and tired, but her eyes were open. "Oh, Mom, you look so much better," Amy said, taking her hand.

"I think I feel better," Nancy murmured.

"You *think*?"

She smiled weakly. "I can't remember how I felt before."

"What *do* you remember?"

Her mother closed her eyes, and for a moment Amy thought she was out again, but then her eyes fluttered open. "The picnic. We were at a picnic in the woods. You and me and Brad. Fried chicken . . ."

"That's right," Amy said.

"It was good chicken," Nancy said thoughtfully. "I don't usually like fried foods, but it wasn't greasy at all."

"It was very good," Amy agreed.

"Brad cooks very well," Nancy murmured.

"Yes."

Some of the fog seemed to clear from Nancy's eyes. "The wine. Oh my God, he tried to poison me, didn't he?"

"Yes."

"He's one of them."

Amy was about to nod but her mother's eyes closed. She was sleeping again.

Amy returned to the Morgans' just as Tasha was coming home from gymnastics. "How is your mother?" Tasha asked.

"Better," Amy said.

"That's good."

"Yes." Then Amy asked, "How was gymnastics today?"

"Not bad. Jeanine tripped on her approach to the vault."

"I'll bet she was embarrassed."

"No kidding."

The girls exchanged knowing smiles that lasted for about half a second. It was nice to have a reminder of their old relationship, even though the reminder was fleeting. *Will we ever have our old friendship back?* Amy wondered longingly.

The theater where the ballet was being performed was big and grand, with chandeliers overhead and plush red velvet seats. Mrs. Morgan's tickets were great—first row, first balcony, where no one could block their view of the stage. The place was packed, and Amy doubted that there was one empty seat.

There wasn't time to look at the program she'd been given. The lights began to dim. Just before the auditorium went completely dark, she and Tasha exchanged smiles that were actually more excited than polite. The beautiful music began. And then the curtain went up.

Immediately Amy felt swept away, as if she too was part of the Christmas festivities displayed on the stage. She was caught up in the color, the movement, the music, and the whole fantasy story of Marie and her nutcracker toy.

Some of the people in the balcony, including Mrs. Morgan, were using binoculars to get a clearer, closer view of the dancers and the sets. With her supersharp vision, Amy didn't need binoculars. Her eyes darted all over the stage as she tried to absorb every detail of the elaborately decorated Christmas tree and the characters who danced around it.

But her eyes stopped darting when they focused on Marie. It wasn't the fancy pink party dress that caught her attention, or the sparkling tiara, or the delicate movements of the slender young dancer. It was her face.

It wasn't an unusual face. Not beautiful or ugly or outstanding in any way. Marie had brown hair and brown eyes and she looked like an ordinary girl. Just like Amy. *Exactly* like Amy. In fact, the ballerina on the stage could be her identical twin!

When she regained her composure, Amy opened her program and fumbled frantically through the pages until she reached the list of performers. It was dark, and she had to strain to make out the name of the dancer. She saw the letter *A* and caught her breath.

When she was able to make out the whole name, she saw that it wasn't Amy—it was Annie. Annie Perrault. She realized that a French girl wouldn't be called Amy. But Annie was pretty close.

Amy's eyes were riveted to the ballerina's face. Her

hair was styled for the performance and she was in costume, but there was no denying that she and Amy looked alike. The performance flew by—the Sugarplum Fairy, the mice, the prince . . . nothing meant anything to her but Marie. Annie. The name didn't matter. What Amy was seeing was another Amy.

With a start she realized the audience was applauding. The performance was over. Dimly she heard Tasha say, "Amy, wasn't that incredible?"

"Incredible," Amy whispered. "Excuse me." She squeezed in front of Tasha to get out to the aisle.

"What are you doing?" Tasha asked.

But Amy didn't take the time to answer. She made her way to the exit.

Unfortunately some audience members wanted to beat the rush and were leaving even as the dancers were still bowing. Amy got caught in the crush, and all the pushing and shoving didn't help get her out of the auditorium any faster.

Eventually she did get outside, where she found herself under a drizzling sky. She ran around to the side of the building. When she spotted a door labeled Stage Entrance, she stopped. Parked on the street nearby was a bus labeled Le Ballet de Jeunesse. Taking a deep breath, Amy went to the stage door and pushed on the handle.

The door opened, but a man in a uniform blocked her way. "What do you want?" he asked sharply.

"I need to see one of the dancers," Amy said.

"You can't come in here," the man said. "This area is only for authorized personnel."

"But it's important!" she pleaded. "It's—it's a matter of life and death!"

He wasn't impressed. "Then you can wait outside till the dancers leave."

"But it's raining!"

He didn't care. Amy was forced to wait outside. The rain wasn't heavy but it was steady, and she was getting wet. She didn't feel it, though. She was too excited at the thought of actually coming face-to-face with another Amy. A sister, in a way.

She recalled Mrs. Morgan saying that the young ballerina was exceptional, an unusually talented dancer. But of course she'd be! Just like Amy could be the best at gymnastics or ice-skating if she wanted to be, this other Amy would be an extraordinary ballerina.

She caught her breath. The door was opening. Two guys came out, rapidly talking to each other in French. They both climbed onto the bus.

Then a group of girls emerged, but the ballerina wasn't with them. Ducking under umbrellas, they ran to the bus. A couple of burly men appeared, carrying the Christmas tree that had been on the stage. They put it into a truck that was parked alongside the bus.

When a young woman emerged and saw Amy, she was taken aback. "Annie? *Qu'est-ce que tu fait ici?*"

Thank goodness Amy had been taking French at school. She knew the woman had mistaken her for Annie and was asking what she was doing outside.

"*Je ne suis pas Annie,*" Amy said carefully. Then, in case the woman knew English and Amy wasn't saying the French correctly, she added, "I am not Annie. *Où est Annie?* Where is Annie?"

The woman gave a shrug that clearly indicated that she didn't know. As she continued onto the bus, she looked back over her shoulder and gave Amy a curious glance.

When she heard the next person come out call "Good night, Joe," to the doorman, she rushed up to him. "Excuse me, sir. I'm looking for someone. Do you know Annie Perrault, the dancer?"

"No, I'm the auditorium custodian," the man said. He held his umbrella so Amy could be covered too. This friendly gesture encouraged her.

"Could I ask you a big favor?" she asked. "Could you take me inside?"

"Sorry," the man said. "That's not permitted." He must have seen the disappointment on Amy's face, because he said, "I'll go back in and find her. What's her name again?"

"Annie. Annie Perrault."

"What does she look like?"

Amy hesitated. "Like me."

The man looked puzzled but nodded and went back.

The rain stopped. Amy was soaking wet and feeling a chill, but she didn't care. She felt like she was about to explode with excitement and anticipation. What should Amy say to her? What would Annie say when she saw Amy? Did Annie know everything that Amy knew?

The door opened and the man came out. "Sorry, honey," he said to Amy. "She's gone."

Amy blinked. "What?"

"She's already left the auditorium."

"But that's not possible!" Amy exclaimed. "I've been standing out here since the ballet ended! She was still on the stage when I left!"

"She must have gone out the other exit," he said. "On the other side of the building."

Amy didn't even thank him for his efforts as he walked away. She was devastated.

It was too much. All that anticipation, all the excitement that had been building up in her, the events of the past few days, the frustration of the moment—it all came out in a rush of sobs. Her tears flowed into the raindrops that were streaming down her face.

"Amy! Amy!" Tasha called. A second later she and Eric were by Amy's side.

Eric was aggravated. "What are you doing out here? Why did you run off like that?"

Amy just shook her head. She couldn't say anything. She couldn't stop crying either.

"I saw her," Tasha said.

Amy looked up. "What?"

"The ballet dancer who looked like you. I could see her through my mother's binoculars. That's why you came out here, didn't you? To find her?"

Amy nodded. Eric was stunned. "You mean, you saw another—" He caught himself just in time.

Tasha looked at him and then at Amy. "Amy, what's going on?"

Amy wiped the tears from her eyes. She looked at her oldest friend, who was gazing at her with the kind of concern that could come only from someone who loved you.

Amy couldn't go on like this. She couldn't keep her secret from Tasha either. From way in the back of her mind, she recalled something her mother had once said to her. "A joy shared is twice the joy, a problem shared is half the problem."

This problem of hers was big. She needed more people to share it. Her mother would have to understand.

"Tasha . . . I'm going to tell you my big secret."

thirteen

Amy tuned out the voice of the swimming instructor and thought about Tasha's reaction the night before. Just like Eric, Tasha hadn't been horrified or grossed out; and she'd believed every word of Amy's story. Amy had to smile as she recalled Tasha's comment. "So *that's* why you never get any cavities." Tasha had sighed in envy; her fear of dentists was well known.

It had been difficult not talking in the car on the way home, but they'd all agreed that the Morgan parents—as well as everyone else on earth—should be kept in the dark as to Amy's special condition. Mrs. Morgan hadn't questioned their silence. She'd assumed they were all dumbstruck by the ballet.

But once home, the three of them had gathered in Tasha's room and talked for hours. By the time she went to sleep, Amy felt sure that with friends like Tasha and Eric, she could deal with all the dangers and bad guys in the world.

"Relay races! Get into your lanes!" Amy had to come back to the present. She joined the two girls she'd been assigned to swim relays with. Amy would go third.

The teacher blew her whistle and the race began. Everyone in level five swam well, so the race was close. But Amy's team was particularly good. The first girl had a lot of power to her kick and established a one-length lead by the time her teammate dove into the pool. This second swimmer wasn't as strong, but she returned just slightly ahead of the girl in the next lane.

Amy was poised, ready to take off. Right next to her, Jeanine was poised too. She glanced at Amy, and Amy could see the tension in her rival's eyes. Obviously she was remembering Amy's performance in the pool on Saturday.

They took off at the same time. Jeanine stroked furiously. Even so, Amy knew how easy it would be to win. And Jeanine had been so awful to her lately, she deserved to be humiliated in front of the whole class.

But then Amy thought about her mother. She thought of Dr. Jaleski. She thought about the friends who now shared her secret—which meant they could be in danger themselves. It wouldn't do anyone any good for her to call attention to herself. It *could* do harm. Slowing herself to a normal pace, she let Jeanine win for her team.

Jeanine didn't appreciate this. Amy saw her after school while she was waiting for Tasha. "You know, Amy, that class may be too advanced for you," Jeanine said. "Maybe you should ask the teacher to bring you back down a level."

Amy did her best to ignore this, though she knew this new patience of hers wouldn't last forever. Tasha came along and Jeanine smiled at her.

"Want to come to the mall with me and Linda?" she asked Tasha.

"No," Tasha said. "I'd rather go home with my best friend."

Jeanine's face fell. "Oh, Tasha, come with us."

Tasha rolled her eyes. "Oh, Jeanine, give it up. Eric's not interested in you, so you can stop being interested in me." With that, she linked arms with Amy and they walked away.

"What a beast," Tasha muttered.

"Totally," Amy agreed happily.

"Your mother's a very strong woman," a nurse told Amy.

No kidding, Amy thought. Strong in more ways than

one. A man she thought she loved tried to kill her, and she isn't even heartbroken.

The nurse made Nancy take a wheelchair out to Mrs. Morgan's car. Amy followed them. They were passing through the hospital lobby when she noticed someone familiar standing in a shadow by the door. While the nurse, her mother, Mrs. Morgan, and Tasha went outside, Amy stopped.

"Mr. Devon? Is that you?"

The former assistant principal stepped out of the shadow. "Hello, Amy."

"What are you doing here?" Amy asked. "Why did you leave Parkside?"

He responded with a question of his own. "Did you enjoy the ballet, Amy?"

She was taken aback. How did he know she'd gone to the ballet? Had he seen her there? Before she could formulate a question, he walked away and disappeared among the throng of people in the hospital lobby.

Amy joined her mother and the Morgans in the car. Her mother took her hand and squeezed it. Amy squeezed back.

"We'll miss having Amy with us," Mrs. Morgan chirped.

"Thank you so much for taking care of my baby," Nancy said.

"*Mom.*"

Nancy ignored that. "She told me you all went to the ballet. That must have been lovely. And terribly expensive. You must let me reimburse you."

"Actually it didn't cost me anything at all," Mrs. Morgan said.

"Really?"

"Yes, the tickets were a gift."

"From who?" Tasha asked.

Mrs. Morgan chuckled. "Actually, I'm not sure. They came in the mail, but there was no note with them. I have a feeling they were from your Great-aunt Eloise, Tasha. It would be just like her to forget to include a note. I'll have to call her this weekend."

Amy sank back in her seat and closed her eyes. It made perfect sense. Tasha's great-aunt hadn't sent the tickets, Mr. Devon had. That was why he knew she'd been to the ballet. He had wanted her to see Annie Perrault. That was also why the seats were so good—an unobstructed view, to be sure Amy could see the ballerina.

But why? And what was she supposed to do now?

Tasha was looking at her with a question in her eyes. Amy mouthed *later* and Tasha nodded. What a relief it was knowing she'd be able to talk over her thoughts instead of keeping them to herself.

Once home, Amy helped her mother upstairs to rest. Coming back down, she heard a knock at the door.

She was more careful now; she looked through the peephole. Mary Jaleski was standing on the doorstep.

Amy opened the door. "Hello. My mother's upstairs."

"It's you I came to see," Mary said.

"Oh! Please, come in."

"I can only stay a moment," Mary told her. "I really shouldn't even be here. It's not safe for me."

A huge lump formed in Amy's throat, and she knew she was on the verge of tears. "I'm so sad that your father died. I didn't know he had a bad heart."

"He didn't have a bad heart," Mary told her. "That's not why he died." She paused. "He was shot, Amy. Someone killed him."

Amy gasped. "Killed? You mean I killed him. He was killed because of me."

"No, Amy," Mary said sharply. "It wasn't your fault. I'm only telling you this because you need to know the kind of danger that exists." Her tone softened. "I know you cared about my father, and he cared about you. I'm glad you two were able to meet."

"I'll never forget him," Amy said. She started to cry.

"I have something for you," Mary said. "Something my father made for you. He'd want you to have it. He didn't have a chance to give it to you himself." She reached into her bag and took out a small piece of tissue.

Amy unwrapped it carefully. On a delicate silver chain hung a small crescent moon. It was the same size and shape as the mark on her back. "It's beautiful," she whispered.

"This is so you will never forget who you are. That's what he told me. I have to go now, Amy. Maybe we'll meet again someday."

Alone in the living room, Amy gazed at the little crescent moon lying in her hand. She wasn't sure if it was the beauty of the charm or knowing who had created it that made it so special. But as she held it to her neck and fastened the chain, she knew she would never take it off.

No matter what Mary had said, Amy knew Dr. Jaleski had died for her. She decided she wouldn't tell her mother. Not now.

As she admired her pendant in a mirror, Amy felt an extraordinary sadness; but at the same time, she had a feeling that everything was going to be okay. She thought about Annie Perrault, and she knew someday they'd meet. Somehow she'd find the other Amys too, whatever their names were now, and they'd be able to help each other. She would learn to channel her skills and her talents so they'd be useful and worthwhile.

There was so much she could do if she put her mind and her body to work. And if she could keep her enemies from interfering with her life.

Amy fingered the crescent moon around her neck. She felt like she had a lucky charm now, a special token that would protect her and give her hope. Dr. Jaleski had made this for her so she would never forget who she was.

As if she ever could.

Memo from the Director

1. The agent has been unsuccessful in the attempt to obtain the subject. This is a minor setback. Efforts will continue, and a new plan is being formulated. The subject remains under surveillance.

2. There is evidence of the existence of another Amy.

Dont miss Replica #3 Another Amy

Perfect Amy Candler tries hard to blend in with everyone else, but then she comes face to face with someone who looks just like her—someone who is another Amy. The two girls look identical, and Amy expects them to have identical personalities. But she's in for a big surprise.

The other Amy is determined to stand out from the crowd.

She's determined to grab the spotlight, even if it means squashing the competition.

She's determined not to have a look-alike, and she wants Amy out of the way.

She's . . . well . . . evil!

Amy must stop her, if she can.

Coming Soon!

We're all different. Or are we?

#1

#2

#3

Amy Candler knows she's different. In fact, she's perfect—a perfect 12-year-old girl. Overnight she can see, hear, and do things better than anyone else and she even knows the answer to every question her teachers ask.

But Amy doesn't have the answers to the mystery of her past. All she knows is that her recurring nightmare seems so real. That her cresent-shaped birthmark wasn't there yesterday. That a strange man is taking photos of her. That her mother is acting weird. That someone is sending her notes to keep her talents a secret.

Slowly Amy is piecing together her identity, but she'd better hurry. . . .

A thrilling new series based on today's headlines.
On sale now wherever books are sold.

Bantam
Bantam Doubleday Dell

BFYR 196